I0720812

THE FINE LINE

TINA BAUER

This book is dedicated to the man who is the complete opposite of Heck Addams: My Husband.

Thank you for all of your support and love. I truly would not be where I am today without you.

I.

There was nothing but noise at first. Crunching metal and screeching brakes. Glass shattering and people screaming. I might have grunted. I did not think I had time to yell. And then it was dark.

It felt like floating, surrounded by this vast emptiness. I tried to think of what could be happening to me, but I was consumed by bleakness. I had no notion of time. No concept of being. I did not exist and yet I was aware that I did not exist.

Then, there was light. It was a thin sliver of pink. Was it something on the horizon in the distance? Or was I imagining it? It all felt surreal. The light grew thicker, ever so slowly taking over the darkness. It turned to different shades of purple, like a majestic psychedelic sunset.

From the center, the silhouette of a feminine figure appeared, small in the distance. She grew larger as she drew closer. She wore a long, black, flowing robe that seemed to float about her in slow motion. Her dark hair was wild around her head, also floating as if she was underwater. Her face was shadowed, but I could see her smile. It was more of a grin. It seemed almost playful.

"Hello, Heck," she spoke, her teasing yet melodic voice echoed through my space. "Do you know where you are?"

I tried to speak, but I could not find my voice. I did not have a throat to speak from. I did not have a tongue or lips to form my words. I did not have anything. Just my being. She floated there, patiently, in the distance, waiting for my response.

"Heaven?" I finally spoke, but not with a voice. It came through from the smallest corner of my mind, barely a whisper.

"Not quite," she giggled.

"Hell," I said, not surprised.

"No. Not that either. At least, not yet," she laughed. "But I have no doubt you will end up there."

There was something malicious about this being. Her voice had a chime to it, reverberating through the emptiness that surrounded us. Under it, there was a sing-song tone as if she was mocking me. I did not know what to make of it.

"Am I dead?" I finally asked, trying to remember how I ended up in this pink and purple nightmare.

"You will be," she sang out. "Think, Heck. You can remember what happened."

I don't know if it was my recollection or something she imprinted on me, but images flooded me.

I could smell the cigarette smoke fill my nostrils and taste the beer and whisky on my taste buds. I could feel the beat of the music vibrating through my body as I made my way to the bar's bathroom.

I was already stumbling a bit, but I made it to a stall. I could handle this. It was not the first time I had left a neighborhood bar drunk. I just needed a little pick-me-up to clear my head and set myself steady. I pulled the little sack of twisted plastic wrap out of my cigarette pack. I opened it carefully, so I would not spill the white powder, and, with my car key, I scooped some up and held it to my nostril. Blow, coke, lines, it did not matter what we called it, it was my best friend for the most part. I took a deep, large sniff and felt it shoot up with a familiar, numbing shock. I repeated the process with the other nostril before pinching my nose for a third and final sniff, shaking my head, and opening my drunken eyes wide. I felt better. Drunk, but alert.

I walked back out to the bar area. It was not crowded. This was a seedy neighborhood bar, all dark and wooden, that made their money from the local alcoholics and occasional under-agers. I tossed a few singles on the bar and announced I was out for the night. No one stopped me.

I walked up the block, not bothering to zipper up against the chilly midnight air and found my car where I parked it. I climbed into the beat-up, old Dodge that I always said I would fix up but never did. I put the key in the ignition and then drove off. Drunk and wired.

I do not know what happened next. I know I was lighting a cigarette and I was in my groove. Someone got in the way. Another car. Maybe more than one car. There were bright lights and the roaring noise of machinery and metal clashing and crumpling.

And then I was here.

"I was in an accident," I said to this floating figure. Who was she? Was she an angel? The Grim Reaper? God?

"You caused an accident, Hector Addams."

It was not the first time I may or may not have caused an accident. If she was my guardian angel, she had not have been watching too closely. I was not exactly the epitome of a fine human being.

"You don't care?" she asked curiously.

"Not in any pain. Just want to know where I am or what is next."

"The pain will come," she grinned. "And you will decide what is next for you. Remember, you are not dead…yet."

This bitch was getting on my nerves. She was so dramatic.

"You have unfinished business, Heck," she continued. "You need forgiveness. You need so much forgiveness. And that will decide where you will go. Will it be heaven for you? Or hell? Will it be eternal love for you? Or nothing but hate?"

"Stop being so Goddamn cryptic," I snapped. Part of me instantly regretted my tone of voice, though I was never one to hold back on what I had to say. I did not know if I should be terrified and yet, I had nowhere to go. I was at her mercy, a bodiless soul imprisoned in an endless and disorienting void.

"It's very simple, Heck. You will awake from your unconscious state—"

"Is that what this is? I'm unconscious?" I cut her off.

"You will awake," she continued, ignoring me. "And you will have a mere five days to find the ones you have hurt the most. You will search deep within yourself and learn about the hurt you've caused. Whether or not you feel remorse is entirely up to you. But then, you will need to beg for their forgiveness."

For the first time, I was at a loss for words. The purple nothingness that surrounded us began to shift. Pink hues created enormous cloud-like images. They moved ever so slightly, like cartoons in slow motion. Their faces turned and revealed themselves to me. I could see them even though they were made of nothing but air, mist, and fog. One of them I barely remembered. But the other four? They filled me with anger. Heather McCully. Brenda Wilson. Julia Collins. Melissa Bracco. Lilith Patton.

Five girls. Five women that I hurt one way or another. Five women that made me miserable in some way or another. There was nothing I could do but chuckle at the fuckery of it all.

"Find them and seek forgiveness," she said.

"Well, fuck," I sighed. I really did not want to talk to any of them. "And if I don't? Or if they don't forgive me?"

She began to laugh. It started as a low, cackle growing louder and harsher, ringing with evil. It filled my being and engulfed my soul. The colors around us seemed to match her mood, changing from purple to yellow, then orange and red resembling fire. It flickered and flashed, but I could not look away. I could not cover my ears to drown out the noise. I did not exist.

"Hell for all of your eternity!" she screeched. "It's all hell for you, Hector Addams!"

I gasped; a scream stuck in my throat as I jumped. I could feel my physical body jerk and I sat up. I was in bed. A hospital bed. I had stickers on my chest with wires attached, an I.V. in one arm, and a blood pressure cuff wrapped around the other. There was a metal handcuff connecting my wrist to the bedrails.

And then the pain hit. My face throbbed and when I breathed in, my left side burst with pain.

"The fuck!" I yelled. This was my voice. It was real. It came from my throat. I reached up with my free hand and felt my face. Gingerly, with my fingertips, I discovered stitches in my lip and some sort of bracing on my nose. Sighing, I laid back down. This was nothing surprising to me. Being banged up comes with the life I lived. Stitches, broken bones, and bruises were all too common to me.

I heard the curtains pull back and who I assumed was a doctor and a nurse walked in, looking at a clipboard. I spotted a pair of police officers out in the hallway.

"Good to see you awake, Mr. Addams," the doctor said.

I laid my head back down, trying to unscramble my mind. There was too much to take in. He checked my vitals.

"Do you know why you are here?" he asked, looking into my swollen eyes with his penlight.

"Car accident," I grumbled.

"Hmmm…your tox report came back pretty loaded," he informed me with judgment in his eyes. I've seen that look before. It wasn't my first time at the DUI rodeo.

"I bet."

The doctor frowned and jotted some things down. He couldn't

be bothered with me. He had real patients to see. I was just another junkie without insurance taking up his time and bed.

"Hey, doc," I called out before he left the room. "What's the damage?"

"You'll survive. You have a broken rib, a broken nose, and split your lip pretty good. You are going to find it painful to walk too. Banged your knee up."

"Way to have good bedside manners," I mumbled. This made the doctor turn around and look at me. He was still judging me.

"Look," he sighed. "You are how old? Twenty-three? This isn't your first time here because of foolish decisions. I doubt it will be your last. I see too many patients like you. Wasting your lives away and don't even care what you are doing to yourself. You can get your act together. You still have a whole life ahead of you. Though, I have no doubt you are already thinking about how and where you are going to score your next fix."

I sighed as they walked out of the room. He wasn't wrong. I was already thinking about my next fix, as he put it. I needed something for the pain. I needed something to take the edge off of being alive. I saw the cops peeking my way and I remembered my wrist was cuffed to the bed.

"Shit," I mumbled to myself. I wondered if they found the blow in my cigarette pack. Or the pipe in my glove compartment. I ransacked my brain, trying to remember what else I might have had in my car, some old empty beer cans and bottles. I might have forgotten or dropped some drugs over time. If they combed the car, I had no doubt they would find a rock or two. Maybe more. Fuck.

The police officers approached me. They were nondescript, looking like every other police officer I have ever dealt with in my life. Just minions in blue, their silver badge taunting and winking from their chests. I rolled my eyes and groaned, turning my head away from them.

"We have some questions, Mr. Addams," one spoke. I knew better. I had to stay quiet.

"Are you aware of the accident you were in?" the other one asked. I lifted my cuffed wrist and jingled it with annoyance like the asshole I am. I knew they were well aware that I was aware. I may or may not have caused the accident due to my tox screening results, but I was not acknowledging anything verbally. I was not stupid.

"You are going to stay cuffed," the taller officer said. "And when the doctors release you, you are coming straight with us to central booking. Unless you want to start talking and answering some questions."

"Excuse me!" A woman's voice spoke from behind them. "Mr. Addams is entitled to a lawyer, and he is way too smart to be answering your questions!"

The voice was familiar, but I could not place it. The officers turned around, moving to the side to let her in. She was dressed in a black skirt and blue blazer. Her plain jane dark heels click-clacked on the cold linoleum floor and she carried a briefcase which she placed on my tray table. Her black hair was pulled into a neat bun, with curls purposefully escaping down the side of her face. Her violet eyes seemed to sparkle as if she was taking delight in my predicament. I could not place where I knew her from. She was not the type of person I would normally associate with. I was a jeans, t-shirt, and work boots kind of guy. She was too clean-cut. People that dressed like her didn't hang around people like me.

She opened the briefcase and pulled out a card, handing it to the officers.

"I'm Hector's lawyer," she announced.

"You are?" I asked, confused. I could not understand where she came from. Even if my family was notified of my accident, I doubted they cared enough to arrange legal counseling. In any case, we couldn't even afford it.

"The county appointed me, Mr. Addams," she informed me before looking back at the officers and handing them some legal documents.

She began a spiel filled with legal jargon that went way over my head. She was stern and confident with the officers as I just lay there quietly trying to understand what was going on. I heard something about having rights as an addict and alcoholic. She stated some sections with numbers and documents that entitled charges to be put on hold until I finished detox.

Some of it felt familiar. I had gone down the detox route before. It kept a lot of restraint to keep from rolling my eyes when she mentioned it. Detox was not for me.

There was some rebuttal from the officers, but she held firm. They knew she had them cornered. For whatever rules and regulations worked in my favor, the cuff came off grudgingly, and they left. She walked behind them, shutting the door so we were alone in the room.

"Glad that's over," she said, walking back to the bed. "Anything I can get you, Heck?"

She sounded and looked so familiar, especially her smile. There was something about the way it bordered on being a loving, friendly smile and a teasing, spiteful grin, but I just could not place her. Maybe I went to school with her back in the day. Or she was from the neighborhood. Her eyes said more though, as if we were more intimate. I wondered if she was someone I met at a local bar and had too much fun with. It was very possible. I had a lot of fun, empty nights.

"I could use some pain meds and a smoke," I admitted.

"Wow," she laughed. "No 'thank you' for getting you some time away from jail? No asking about the other people in the accident? If they are alive? You really are a self-centered son of a bitch, aren't you?"

"What the fuck?"

"There's no time for you to get all big and bad," she grinned. "The clock has just started ticking. They will be coming soon to escort you to the detox ward. You have to get out of here if you want to complete the list."

"The list?" I was so confused. What the hell was she babbling about?

"Who are you?"

"Oh, I'm sorry. Here. Maybe this will help." She reached into her pocket and pulled out a business card, handing it to me.

Instead of her name and her lawyer's information, it was a list. A list of five names.

Heather McCully
Brenda Wilson
Julia Collins
Melissa Bracco
Lilith Patton

It all came back to me. The nothingness. The colored lights in the everlasting void. Her.

"You!" The grin. That evil grin with the cackling laugh.

"In the flesh!" she laughed. "But seriously, get your shit together and get out of here. What did the doc say about you having your whole life ahead of you? Yeah…you don't. The clock to your death has begun. Five days. At the stroke of midnight at the end of your fifth day, you will die, and your fate will be sealed. It's heaven or hell for you."

"Are you my guardian angel?" I had to know.

"Oh, fuck no."

"Then why are you helping me? You could have just let them arrest me."

"Because I love some good drama," she sneered. "But from here on in, you are on your own. Tick Tock, Motherfucker."

And just like that, she was gone. She left me in a state of confusion. She was so different when we first met in that other world of nothingness. She was a spirit of sorts, celestial. But now, she appeared human in both body and manner. And the worst of it all was she seemed to be enjoying my predicament.

I looked at the clock above the dry-erase board. It was 1:35 in the afternoon. On the board, a nurse had written her name and the date. Tuesday, November 2nd, 1993. I had until Saturday at midnight to determine my everlasting fate.

The room swerved and pain shot down my leg from my knee as I tried to get out of bed. I steadied myself, realizing I would need something to get me through this. A bottle of something. A hit of anything.

I hobbled to the narrow closet and pulled out some clothes from a plastic bag with the hospital's logo on it. They were not mine, but they were my size. Something told me this was the doing of that bitchy angel or spirit or whatever the fuck she was. There was no one else in my life that would have taken care of me like that. I doubted anyone even knew I was in an accident and if they did, they didn't care. I figured if she could pretend to be a lawyer and pull me out of this mess, she could somehow manifest some clothes for me. One thing I knew for sure, anything was possible with this chick. I didn't know if that frightened me or excited me.

The clothes that I was wearing the night before were cut off from me and tossed. It's what they did in the ER when one was unconscious. I've seen it before with friends. Somehow, my leather jacket was saved. It hung on the hook. I was glad to see that. The jacket was one of the few possessions that I treasured. Again, I wondered if she had anything to do with saving my jacket.

I carefully dressed. I found my wallet at the bottom of the bag. I grabbed it and the card with the list of names on it, shoving them in my jacket pocket. I pulled the collar up around my chin as if that was going to disguise me, wishing I had a baseball cap of sorts. I had to leave undetected because they were coming to throw my ass in detox.

I opened my door just a slit and peeked out. Surprisingly, it was not too busy. Even better, my room was away from the nurses' station and close to the elevator. I waited until an elderly couple walked up to the elevator. They were most likely just visitors to a patient, dressed in everyday clothes and winter jackets. The woman's arm was slipped around the man's. They had no authority or title. I put my head down and slipped behind them just when the elevator dinged and opened its doors.

And just like that, I was off my floor, away from the nurses and staff who would recognize me. I rode the elevator in silence, wanting to breathe a sigh of relief. It occurred to me that I was getting away with this too easily. I did not know how much power the dark angel had, and it scared me that she might be making it easier for me. Only because I knew the worst was yet to come. I realized I should have asked questions and demanded answers from her. Part of me wondered if she would have even provided those answers. I doubted it.

I exited the elevator and found a side door that bypassed security. The cold November air hit me, making the pain in my face worse, turning the deep throbbing into a web of stabbing pins and needles from my nose to my cheekbones and up around my brows. Painkillers. I needed painkillers first and foremost. I was aware that my eternity hung in the balance, but first things first.

It took me a moment to remember that I did not have a car. It must have been totaled and towed away. I never asked. Rethinking,

I found a payphone and beeped one of my several connections. I waited for the phone to ring and asked if he was carrying vikes. It was not long before he pulled up and we made the exchange.

I swallowed two pills dry before I tried to think of what I was doing. I could just go home and sleep everything off. That seemed like the logical thing to do. Sleep, then drink and get high. Followed by ignoring just about everything in my life. This whole crazy guardian angel thing had to be a joke. It had to be a figment of my imagination, caused by trauma to my brain with the accident.

I fingered the card in my pocket. It was real and very much present. A list of five names. Five days. I could not possibly take this seriously, and yet…what if it was all real? Was I really going to die by Saturday night? Were these five girls really the decider of my eternal fate? It wasn't the dying that scared me. I've been dying my whole life. It was the hell part. I didn't exactly know what hell meant, but I did know it wasn't good. I could not spend eternity in hell. Earth was hell enough.

I decided it was best to play it safe than sorry. I had to come up with a plan of how I was going to get to the first name on my list: Heather McCully. She was an easy one to find. I knew where to find her. It was just a matter of getting there. And the whole forgiveness nonsense.

I saw a bus stop across the street and decided that was the only way to go. It was miles from where she lived. I could have walked it, on a better day. Plus, here was the whole pressed-for-time nonsense.

The bus took a little longer than I would have liked to arrive. I dropped some loose change in the fare box just as the Vicodin began to cloud my mind. The wonderful, buzzing warmth reached out and relaxed my limbs and face as I walked to the back of the bus and sat down on a bench.

I leaned my head on the window, gazing out the window, seeing the streets of my town pass on by. Garden Hollows was an exit town, sitting right off the interstate. It's a small town of nobodies. Many weary travelers come to spend the night or grab a meal and gas, but no one ever stays. And those of us that were unlucky enough to be born here hardly ever leave.

The scenery from the bus window slowly began to fade away. At first, I thought it was the Vicodin over-doing its thing and mixing with whatever was still in my system from the night before, but then I realized it was something that was beyond any control. It was more than a high. It was a fog that settled around me, erasing the bus, its smells, and sounds. It was taking me back to a distant memory. A memory of Heather.

The fog lifted as quickly as it settled. I was no longer on the bus but rather back at my house. I realized I was also back about a year or so when Heather and I were together.

Heather and I started dating for all the wrong reasons. It only took a few weeks before she moved in with me at my mother's house. Technically, it was my parents' house, but does a father count when he's doing time in a state penitentiary? Since my mother spent most of her time at the bar or crashed on the living room couch, Heather and I took over the master bedroom.

It was a Saturday night and I had just come out of the bathroom, my long hair wet from the shower. I looked at myself in my bedroom mirror as I brushed my hair back. I looked like most guys from my town. Average. Brown hair. Brown eyes. Just a touch of facial hair on the chin and upper lip. Better looking than some. Not as good-looking as others. I was in pretty decent shape, considering the very unhealthy lifestyle I lived. I was still young though. I knew soon enough the smoking and drinking would cause wrinkles before its time. The unhealthy eating would settle around my middle. My teeth would eventually get yellow and my hair was just a mere couple of years away from thinning. Eventually, I would look like every other middle-aged citizen of Garden Hallows.

I turned around to see Heather laying on an old beanbag chair held together with duct tape in the corner. She was curled up, her knees to her chest, whimpering. We fought just before I took my shower. Now, she was using her pathetic tactics to make me feel bad. It was not going to work. I just wanted to finish getting ready and have a good time.

My brother, Freddie, and our friend Mitch were sitting on the bed, a record album cover on the end table with lines prepped and ready to be snorted. I did my two lines then turned on my stereo to blast Metallica's latest hit. I dug into my disheveled drawers to find some jeans and a T-shirt.

"What's with her?" Freddie asked as I went to the bathroom to finish getting dressed.

"Who the fuck knows," I admitted. Heather was always moody. She was a beautiful girl with a head full of frosted curls, a light spray of freckles across her nose and cheeks, and big blue eyes. She always smelled so fresh and clean, no matter how much she smoked or drank. She had a squeaky mouse of a voice that bordered between cute and adorable or whiny and annoying. Lately, it was more on the whiny and annoying side.

"You gonna get ready?" I asked, walking back into the room, and lighting up a cigarette.

"I told you," she sniffled. "I don't want to go."

"So, you just gonna sit around here and hang with my deadbeat mom?" I half-heartedly joked. I did not know what her problem was, and I did not care either. I just wanted to head out and have as much of a good time as I could have in this godforsaken town.

"Please, Heck," she cried. "Stay home with me."

"Oh, my god, Heather. Get the fuck up off the floor! You are embarrassing me! Come on! Just get dressed and come out with us!"

She pulled herself together and stood up. Her blue eyes were red.

Whether it was from crying or all the weed she smoked earlier, I did not know. And again, I did not care.

She walked up to me, her face inches from mine. She suddenly screamed, taking me off guard.

"FUCK YOU!!"

And then she stormed out of the room. Freddie and Mitch looked bewildered before starting to laugh. I cracked a smile. It was funny hearing that squeaky little voice trying to be so hard. It was hard to take someone who sounded like a cartoon seriously.

I did another two lines as we joked about Heather's sudden outburst until anger crept up on me. How dare she think she can be like that with me? I'm the one that gave her a place to live. I'm the one who paid for her clothes, her food, her drugs, her drinks, and so on. She was the one that chose to live this life with me.

Her voice kept ringing in my head, getting on my nerves. How dare she scream like that in front of my friends. My fists clenched; my jaw tighten.

Before I knew it, I was barreling out of the room and house. I could hear Freddie mumble, "Here he goes." I did not care. Heather needed to be told her place.

I found her up the block, talking to a driver in a white van. I knew that van well and the driver even better. Lilith Patton. She was Heather's cousin and sometimes best friend. Girls changed their best friends with the seasons. Last I heard, they were not on speaking terms, and I was partly to blame. It began right around the time Heather and I became a couple.

Fuck!" I screamed down the block. Lilith just smiled at me. At one time, Lilith and I were friends. The best of friends even. Practically family. Not anymore. Too much history between us. Just the sight of her talking to Heather sent my head reeling.

I knew Lilith as well as I knew myself. She was feeding Heather's empty little head. Telling her lies about me, that I was no good, calling me all sorts of names, and doing it all with a smile on her face.

"Really?" I said, approaching them. I could see Lilith's eyes on my clenched fists. She raised an eyebrow. I immediately relaxed my hands. "Get away from my girlfriend, bitch."

"Get away from my cousin, bastard," she sang back before looking at Heather again. "Look, you know where to find me. I can't be around him."

"Fuck you!" I yelled at her.

"Go to hell!" she fired back before driving away. God, I hated her. I would have punched her van, but she went too quickly.

"Why are you talking to her? You know I hate her!" I turned to Heather, grabbing her by the shoulders and shaking her. It was too much, her whining and embarrassing me, but then to bring Lilith into it. Seeing Lilith put me on a whole different path of anger. It was Lilith I really wanted to shake.

"Heck! Stop! I'm pregnant!!" she screeched. I sucked my breath in like I was slapped.

"What?"

"I'm pregnant," she said, softer, tears rolling down her face.

I let go of her, trying to think. I needed to get away from her because I wanted to hit her. Too much frustration was built up inside of me, my mind swirling with intoxication, and now Heather laid this on me. It was not uncommon for me to unleash emotions with my fist. There were plenty of holes in the walls of my house that were evident of that. I wouldn't hit her though. I was a jackass, but not that much of a jackass. I needed to get away from her, the house, my brother, my friend. I just needed to go. Slamming my fists into my pockets, I turned to walk away.

"Heck?"

"Not now!" I shouted as I continued to walk. This was a common occurrence for me. I would be filled with rage, hate, and confusion,

and I would walk. I sometimes walked for miles. I didn't know why.
I had been doing it since I was a kid. I would walk away and keep
walking until all the emotions subsided or just destroyed everything.
Lilith used to call it my "psycho walk."

The blow was wearing off and I needed a drink. No matter where
you walked in or around Garden Hollows, you could find a hole-in-
the-wall bar. I walked into a generic bar with a generic Irish name.
The place was dark with red vinyl stools and booths, the floors sticky,
the air smoky, and the music from the jukebox loud but slightly
staticky. The crowd was thin, mostly locals and some older men
having their beer and minding their own business. I had been there
hundreds of times before and would be there hundreds of times
more. I was on my third drink, Heather's voice echoing in my brain
when she walked in.

Lilith was with her sisters and some other people from the
neighborhood. She saw me and smiled. I rubbed my head in
frustration. Lilith was unlike any girl I knew. She was the only girl
who was not afraid of my temper. Even my mother became afraid
of me as I got older.

I wanted so badly to punch the smile off of her face, but I knew
better. She had friends with her. Male friends. I was going to keep
myself in check.

Lilith had the gall to walk over and take the empty barstool next to
me. I could have moved or even left, but I didn't. I was curious to see
where this was going, what her deal was. Maybe I was even looking
for an excuse to get into a fight. Fighting with her was a rush. Hating
her got the adrenaline pumping. She waved down the bartender and
ordered some watered-down excuse for a beer.

"I thought you went straight," I said before sipping my whiskey.

"Just the drugs," she said. "No more of that for me."

I rolled my eyes.

"So, should I be congratulating you or what?" she asked.

I looked at her, confused.

"The baby?" she reminded me.

"Fuck. You know?"

"I think everyone knows, Heck. She may act all ditzy, but she's smarter than she lets on. She plays you for a fool," she laughed.

I looked at her. She could see the annoyance on my face. Only Lilith could read the irritation in my eyes when I was like this.

"Oh, calm the fuck down," she continued. "Babies are cute."

"You're jealous," I suddenly realized, smiling.

"Jealous?" she laughed. "Yeah. Okay. Sure."

"Yep. You wish it was you."

She sipped her beer, watching me through the mirror behind the bar. She broke out with the biggest grin.

"Right. I'm jealous…of the youthful days ending. Working hard to only spend money on diapers, formula, and all the other stuff that babies and kids bring," she rambled. "I'm jealous of being forever connected to someone I don't give a shit about. Being in the same relationship with this person for the rest of my life. Raising a baby in my drunk mother's home because there is no way in hell I can afford a baby and a place of my own."

She was speaking the truth. And I was listening, as much as I did not want to.

"And you know damn well it ain't gonna end with just one baby. Another one will pop out in a year or two. And then maybe even a third one. All them crying, sniveling little rug rats. And Heather… Heather is now pretty much your wife, whether you make it official or not," she continued. "Heather, who needs constant attention. Who needs to constantly be reminded of how beautiful she is because let's face it, that girl's self-esteem is in the toilet."

Lilith knew. She grew up with Heather. She had witnessed the very worst of the lovely but fragile Heather.

Lilith suddenly spun towards me on her barstool. She leaned in close, staring into my eyes, making me suddenly uncomfortable. I got a glimpse of the old friend she once was. The friend before we became each other's worst enemies. I had to push those memories away. That friendship could not be rekindled. I refused to let that happen.

"I know you hate me, Heck," she said softly. "But if I can give you one word of advice: Get out while you still can."

And with that, she hopped off her stool and walked back to her friends, not looking back.

I paid for my drink and left. I walked home and noticed Mitch and Freddie were gone. Heather was sleeping in bed. I watched her sleep. She was wearing an old, tattered Led Zeppelin shirt of mine, her hair a mess of curls piled on top of her head and held with one of her many ridiculous scrunchies. It bothered me to see her sleeping soundly while I was out trying to calm the loud, crowded, angry thoughts in my head and getting lectured by Lilith.

I sat on the edge of the bed and looked around. Empty cans and bottles littered the room. Bongs with dirty water sat on the dresser. Razor blades and fast-food straws cut down to the perfect size for snorting were strewn about everywhere. An ashtray overflowed. The room was a complete disaster. Heather could not even be bothered to clean up after us, but we were going to put a baby in this mix?

Lilith was right, too, about babies coming one after another. It was just a thing in our town. Garden Hollows was low-income trash for the most part. The addiction and alcohol rates were through the roof. And yet no one bothered to protect themselves from unwanted babies. It was a vicious cycle. I was not ready to end my cycle either. I liked my ways. I liked drugs. I liked my alcohol. The harder the better. It seemed horrible, but it was true. A baby would just be a burden.

"You have to go!" I yelled, slamming a fist on the bed to wake up Heather. She yelped, confused and startled.

"You need to get your shit and go!" I repeated.

"Wait, Heck—"

"Just go!"

My voice boomed, coming from the pit of my stomach. I could feel the veins popping out of my neck. I could see she felt the anger in my words. I wasn't just my usual angry self, off on some dumb tangent. The force behind two simple words hung in the air, vibrating through the room. She whimpered and jumped out of bed, scrambling as she randomly gathered her things.

"But the baby…" she trailed off, crying.

"Just get rid of it!" I screamed, pushing her out of the room.

I jolted back to reality with the sound of a bus bell ringing and my screams stuck in my throat. There was no room or house. No Heather crying about a baby. It was all gone, nothing but a memory. I was back on the bus with the bus driver and my last words to Heather repeating in my mind.

"Last stop," the bus driver said, pulling over. I blinked a few times, the memories and Vicodin haze lingering. I looked up at the driver. She was smiling at me through the rearview mirror. Her dark hair was pulled back, tucked under her cap. She gave me that sneering smile. It was unmistakable. It was her. And she was very much real, not just something I made up.

I shook my head. Why did I have a feeling that the damn bitch was going to haunt me all week?

"Good luck with Heather," she sang out as I disembarked from the rear door of the bus. That teasing, mocking voice made my skin crawl. I didn't know who this woman was or what she was, but she knew how to get into my head. If she was anyone else, I would have lashed out. Yelling would have ensued. A scene would have been caused. Cursing and spittle would have left my mouth in anger, but I was not sure if it would be wise to antagonize an angel of death or whatever she was.

Heather did get rid of it. And not even two weeks later, she had moved in with Mitch. She was that type of girl. Always needed another guy to love her and take care of her. She just could not be alone and single. Lilith was right about her low self-esteem. She went from my living situation to Mitch's living situation, which was the same. Mitch was better than me, though. While I had no doubt the drugs and drinking were still going on in Heather's life, Mitch was mild-mannered. There was no anger. No sudden rage.

The sun was beginning to set by the time I walked down Mitch's street. I was not surprised to see him in his driveway, head under the hood of his latest knock-around car. Mitch's long blonde hair was pulled through the loop in the back of his baseball cap. His jacket was zipped up to his chin. He saw me approach, put his tool down, and leaned on his car with his arms folded.

"About time someone beat the shit out of you, Dick," he snarled. We were no longer on friendly terms.

"Car accident," I mumbled.

He shrugged, showing he did not care.

"Um…Heather around?" I asked.

"Why?"

"I need to talk to her," I said.

"No," he said, turning his back.

"Look, I'm not here to start anything. I just need to talk to her." How do I tell him that I was dying, and my eternal fate depended on Heather, among others, to forgive me? How do I even begin to explain that I was already a dead man walking and being stalked by some weird spirit that seemed hell-bent on making my final days a nightmare? Or maybe it was all in my head, and I was slowly going mad? I scrambled for a lie.

"I fucked up," I blurted out, letting my mouth ramble about anything that could remotely pass for the truth. "I was in this bad accident, and I realized that I need to get my shit together. I need to go back to detox and meetings and make amends."

Mitch looked at me closely, then snickered.

"Dick, you are high now! Look at your pupils!"

"Mitch, come on. That's just the painkillers they gave me at the hospital. It's prescribed. Totally legit," I half-lied. "I just want to talk to Heather. I owe her an apology. You can be right there with her while I talk to her."

Mitch sighed and shook his head in disbelief. Then he nodded.

"Wait here."

I waited outside, my knee throbbing. The painkillers were already wearing off. I just wanted to go, down a couple of shots, take a couple of hits off my bong, and then drift off to sleep. I leaned on Mitch's car to take some of the weight off my knee.

Mitch came back out with Heather behind him. Her petite and rail-thin frame was swallowed up by one of his sweat jackets. She had a frown on her face, but it softened when she saw my battered face.

"Oh my God," she gasped, her voice sounding cute and squeaky. "Are you okay?"

This was the Heather that made it easy for everyone to fall in love with her. She just wanted to be liked. Even by me, the ex-boyfriend she had not spoken to in about a year. Her concern was genuine.

I touched my face with my fingertips and cast my eyes downward, feeling self-conscious of my stitches and nose. "Yeah, I'm okay. Just a bit banged up. How you doing?"

She shrugged, and all three of us stood there in the driveway, awkwardly.

"Are you going to say something, or are we just gonna look at each other?" Mitch finally said, breaking the silence.

"Yeah, right," I sighed, trying to think. "So…um…like I was telling Mitch, this accident kinda woke me up. I got this lawyer who's gonna help me go straight. Get my shit together. I'm gonna leave in a few days for detox…"

I did not know where the words were coming from. I just snowballed into a whole story of lies.

"Before I leave, there are some things I have to take care of. My lawyer suggested it. You know, make amends," I continued. "And, well, you are on the top of my list. I just wanted to come by and tell you how sorry I am for being a shitty boyfriend—"

"Dick, you were abusive," Mitch reminded me.

"Okay. Can you please stop calling me that?" I asked, annoyed, then looking back at Heather. "He's right though. I was…I am an abusive person. You deserved better. And I should have handled the whole baby situation better. I'm sorry."

Heather looked over at Mitch who shrugged. She wrapped her sweat jacket tighter around her and nodded. I prayed that she didn't see through me and catch on to my act. While everything I spoke out loud was true, I was not feeling the truth. I would never swallow my pride and admit I was wrong or a horrible person. On a normal day, I would never ask for forgiveness. I just hoped she could not see the insincerity in my eyes.

"Okay. Yeah. You sucked," she said. "But I'm okay now. Mitch showed me that I didn't deserve the way you treated me. It's all good now. Things happen for a reason, right?"

I breathed a sigh of relief. I should have realized she would be an easy target. She was always so stupid. Beautiful but stupid.

"Right. Yeah. Exactly," I smiled. "We good?"

"I guess so," she smiled. "So, you going straight now?"

I nodded, knowing I was lying.

"Wow. That's all Lilith ever wanted for you," she said, sadly.

"Well, I guess things happen for a reason, like you said," I said, starting to get annoyed. Why did she even have to bring Lilith up? "Don't worry. Lilith's on my list."

Heather frowned, her brows furrowing, and her bottom lip turned into a sad pout. She glanced at Mitch. He just shook his head and rolled his eyes. I could see there was an unspoken conversation between the two of them. They knew something about Lilith that I didn't, but I didn't bother to question them. When it came to Lilith, I didn't even want to know. There was always drama with that girl. Just talking about her irritated me, so I was not about to start that conversation. It was bad enough that Lilith was on my list. I just wanted to get away from Heather and Mitch. I needed to move on. I would deal with Lilith on my terms. I had no doubt Lilith was at the bottom of my list for a reason. It was saving the worst for last.

"Anyway," I said as I backed away. "I'm going to get out of here and leave you two alone. Gotta rest up. But it was good seeing you two. And thank you. I am starting to feel better about myself."

I turned around and walked down the block. I did not want to see them anymore. I needed to get away before something stupid was said and I ruined all chances of a peaceful fate. I didn't know where that damn angel was, but I knew she was watching and listening closely. I could not take any chances.

I pulled the business card out of my pocket. Heather's name was mysteriously erased. Only four remained. Brenda Wilson, Julia Collins, Melissa Bracco, Lilith Patton. One down, four more to go.

I was exhausted. Between the accident, the painkillers, facing Heather and Mitch, and the whole demon-angel bitch looking over my shoulder, everything took its toll on me. And I was starving. You would think for someone aware of his eminent death and fate laying in the hands of limited time, I would not have an appetite. But I guess the body still needs to function.

The first thing I did when I arrived home was find something to eat in the kitchen. My mother was numbed out on the couch as usual, sitting in the glow of the television. I could hear Fresh Prince rapping about moving to Bel Air as I made myself a meal. A bowl of cereal and a bologna sandwich. God forbid there was a real meal in my house. I could not even remember the last time my mother cooked.

I wolfed down what would classify as garbage, favoring my split lip, then headed to take a shower and crash for the night. It took a couple more pills, a bottle of beer, and a hit from my bong to make the pain go away. I drifted off into a welcoming dark slumber.

I had forgotten to set my clock radio, so by the time I woke up, it was afternoon. It took a minute to remember that I was on a deadline, with emphasis on dead. I shot up and rubbed my head. I pulled on some jeans and groaned as the pain in my knee and ribs reminded me again of the accident.

"Fuck," I groaned, pulling an old concert jersey over my head and then lighting a cigarette. I needed to calm down and think. Who was next? Where did I need to go?

I found the business card on my dresser next to my wallet and an old empty cigarette pack. The four names glared at me. Brenda was next. Brenda Wilson.

Truth be told, I barely remembered who Brenda was. It took me a few long seconds as I tried to remember the faces that were shown to me when I was unconscious in the hospital bed. If it were not for the shape-shifting images that appeared when I was in the depths of that senseless nightmare with *her*, I would be completely clueless as to who Brenda was. Brenda was just some random club girl. I knew her for thirty minutes, give or take. I did not even know her last name was Wilson. I had no clue where she lived.

I racked my brain trying to remember something. Anything. But it was blank. I don't even know how I could have possibly hurt a girl I barely knew, but she was on the list. I had to find her.

I walked into the kitchen to find something to wash down my pills and was somewhat surprised to see my mother awake and making herself coffee. She was in a bathrobe and her hair was all disheveled, but she was awake. She eyed me up and down, pouring a shot of something into her coffee mug.

"The hell happen to you?" she finally asked.

"Car accident."

"Well, that's just great!" she snorted. "Hope they don't sue your ass because you ain't got nothing to give."

"Thanks. By the way, I'm fine."

I rolled my eyes and walked away. I had to get away from her. Sooner or later, she was going to try and pick a fight with me, and I just was not having it. I did not have time to indulge in her pathetic "poor me" drunken episodes where she's this amazing mom and I'm the ungrateful son. And then, somehow my father and brother's name will get thrown in there too.

I glanced out the front window to see Freddie's car parked outside. He was probably sleeping off his own demons. Without thinking twice, I grabbed his keys and left before he would wake up or she started screaming.

I did not know where I was going, but I knew I needed to clear my head. I needed a pick-me-up and coffee just would not do it. Everything seemed heavy and dark, as it usually did when I was sober. First things were first. A payphone to beep someone. Then wait around for him to show up. A quick and easy exchange, and then my mind was cleared with two snorts of blow and that wonderful, almost gagging numbness of a drip down the back of my throat. I was able to think straight again.

I drove around some more, with nothing but the name *Brenda* whispering in my head. I remembered meeting her at a club called Escapades. It was still early in the day, but I decided to head over there and park and wait. It was all I had. Maybe, hopefully, she still frequented this club, and I would catch her walking in when it opened. Or maybe I could wait for it to open and question the bartenders there if they knew her. Either way, I was staking out the place. I didn't have a better idea.

I did a couple of more bumps before putting my head back on the headrest and waited. The blow should have made me wired, but instead, a fuzzy cloud wrapped itself around me, taking me away from the hustle and bustle outside my car. I closed my eyes and shook my head, hoping it would all clear up and go away. It didn't. I opened my eyes to see the images around me swirling as if I was being flushed down a toilet. I was filled with dizzying nausea. And then it all came to an abrupt halt, and everything cleared. The timeline shifted. I was no longer in the comforts of my brother's car. I was in a forgotten memory.

I was inside Escapades with flashing lights and the loud bass of some lame song that plays at every wedding, club, and high school dance was blasting and thumping. Bodies were dancing on the main dance floor almost in unison. I was standing with Mitch and Freddie, my eyes scanning the floor. Lilith had disappeared into the crowd with some preppy loser and for some odd reason that bothered me. She came with us. It was her idea to check out this club. We were bar people, but she insisted the club might be fun. And now she was not even hanging with us. She was off dancing with some guy that was so not her type.

Freddie nudged me and pointed to a group of girls that were looking our way. They were giggly and the type to pretend they did not notice you as soon as you looked at them. They were dressed in the latest styles from whatever Beverly Hills soap opera they most likely watched, not the denim and T-shirt outfits of the girls I usually hung out with. Definitely not our type. But neither was the nerdy jock with the winged, feathery hair and polo shirt Lilith took off with. He looked like he was still stuck in the mid-1980's, ready to go a round or two with *The Karate Kid*.

If Lilith could have her fun, so could I. Who cared if they weren't my type? Though, I knew Lilith would care. Lilith was weird like that.

I ordered a large round of shots and had Freddie and Mitch help me carry them over to the giggly girls. It was an ice breaker and got them to loosen up. The talk was small and honestly quite stupid, but I had a glance at Lilith in the distance, and she was watching. I could tell she was not happy with me. This gave me the incentive to start paying attention to this one bubbly cute girl. Brenda.

Brenda had a big head of golden-brown curls and large green eyes. She was cute enough and tried to play this innocent act with the batting of the eyes and flirtatious giggles. She was babbling about college and trying to sound all intelligent, but I was barely paying attention. I just smiled and nodded, but mostly watched Lilith.

Lilith made her way over to me, her hand pulling Biff or Chip or whatever the fuck his dumb name was, through the crowds. She looked Brenda up and down then turned to me and grinned.

"Who's your little friend?" she asked. I could see something flashing in Lilith's eyes. I've seen it before. It was jealousy. Her little wheels were turning on how she was going to torture and tease me about Brenda.

"Brenda. This is Lilith." She just continued to look her up and down with judgment. She hated this little college co-ed just as much as I hated the preppy she was with.

"Good luck," Lilith laughed before grabbing a shot, downing it, then pulling the guy back on the dance floor. I was beginning to feel bad for the poor sap.

"What did she mean by that?" Brenda asked, standing close to me, shouting in my ear over the music.

"Who the hell knows? Lilith plays games. Ignore her," I shouted back. It was true. Lilith always played games. And I played games back.

I could see Lilith was still watching us as she danced closely with her guy. I slipped my hand around Brenda's lower back and pulled her closer to me, my face in her hair.

"You smell really good," I told her as she giggled and blushed.

"You too," she said. Nothing original there.

I looked over and saw that Lilith was kissing the guy. I did not know why but it made my blood start to boil. Why did I care so much? She was supposed to be hanging with us not getting her rocks off with some random jerk. We were supposed to be in one of our usual hangouts listening to good tunes and just chilling, not in this overcrowded, sweaty, loud cesspool of hormones.

I looked back down at Brenda who was beaming up at me. You would think a guy never put their arm around her before. Maybe the night was not a total loss. The conversation lingered between boring and idiotic, nothing but small talk about anything. I wanted to get her to shut up and let things go where they might go.

Lilith was back at my side. She gave me a quick peck and handed me the keys to her van.

"I'm leaving with Tad," she announced. "Take my van? I'll call you in the morning."

Tad. That was his name. It did not surprise me.

And just like that, Lilith was gone. She was off to do whatever it was she was going to do with Tad. I had to take some slow, steady breaths to calm down. Only Lilith could get on my nerves the way she did. That night was her idea. The club was her plan. And then she leaves. She wasn't my girlfriend, and I had no right to be angry. But still, she was being a bitch, playing her little games, and she knew it.

I stared at the keys in my hand. Her keychains jangled together. One was a big "L." The other was a silver metal pot leaf. The third was just a glittery blue and yellow "Make it a Blockbuster Night" slogan.

"You guys must be really close if she trusts you with her car," Brenda said.

"Best friends," I admitted, closing my fist on the keys. I did not want to think about Lilith anymore. Brenda was right there, looking willing and able to have a good time.

"Want to get out of here? Go talk where it's quieter?" I suggested.

"Where?"

"Does it matter? How we gonna get to know each other when we can barely hear each other? Besides, this music kinda sucks. Lilith's got some good cassettes in the van."

Brenda shrugged, her eyes shy and coy. She leaned over to her friends to tell them she was stepping out for a bit. They put on the whole big, concerned friends act, saying things like "no, don't go" and "are you sure" but never actually stopping her. They were still happy to have Mitch and Freddie buy them drinks and keep them occupied.

Outside, the air was cooler and felt good after the hot club. I lit a cigarette and offered Brenda one, but she shook her head. We walked to the parking lot, and I let her in Lilith's van.

Lilith's van was the kind mothers told their children to watch out for. The kind of van you would expect a creepy man luring children into with the promise of candy and puppies.

There were only two seats in the van. The driver's and the passenger's. Anyone else who hitched a ride with Lilith sat on the floor or on plastic, overturned milk crates. Occasionally someone would bring a beach chair to sit in. Not the safest options, but no one cared. The van did its job. It carted us wherever we needed to go.

Lilith also kept some old blankets and pillows in the van. She used these for nights she was too messed up to drive home and would just crash in the van. I spread the blankets out in the back of the van and sat down. Brenda looked nervous and I patted a spot next to me.

"What's wrong? Don't you want to hang?" I asked.

Again, she did that playful shy shrug as if she was unsure of herself. Her cutsie-pootsie act was starting to get annoying. She came down from the passenger seat and sat next to me. I scooted closer to her and put my arm around her shoulder. I could feel her stiffening up.

"So, do you go to school? Or do you work?" she asked, a nervous giggle caught in her throat.

"I work," I reply, playing with her hair, wrapping a curl around my fingers.

"Oh. Then what do you do?"

"I drive a tow-truck."

"Oh. I work too. I'm a cashier at Bargains and Deals. It's a cool place to work. People are nice. Do you like your job?"

Was she just going to babble? I needed to move this along. I did not bring her out to the van to play Twenty Questions.

I leaned in and kissed her. The kiss was soft and gentle. Wanting more, I parted my lips and let my tongue force its way to entwine with hers. It only lasted a second before she jerked back away from me. I frowned at her. Again, she giggled, sheepishly touching her lips with her fingertips.

"Sorry," she said. "I'm just nervous. I never…"

"Are you trying to tell me you are a virgin?" I asked, laughing. She could not be serious.

She shrugged and then nodded. Her eyes cast downward, avoiding my stare. She suddenly went from shy and flirty to appearing as if she was hiding something. As if she was guilty. Of what, I had no clue.

"A virgin? For real?" I said, no longer laughing.

Again, she nodded.

"Do you even want to be here right now?"

"I—I don't know," she said, her eyes wide and bewildered. I pulled away from her.

"You fuckin' serious? Did you really think I invited you out here to talk? We met in a club, not a library. What the fuck did you think was going to happen?"

"This—this is my first time," she said quietly, looking down at her hands.

"What's your first time?" Now I was the confused one.

"Everything."

I did not know what to think. I shook my head and rolled my eyes. I pulled myself up and sat in the driver's seat and lit a smoke. Looking down at her, she looked like a scared little girl.

"You know what you are?" I asked as she shook her head. "A fuckin' tease. Don't be a tease. Either you go to a club and have a good time, or you don't. Don't be all cute and shy and flirty and let a guy think he's got a shot and then just shoot them down. Don't be a fuckin' tease. No one is going to like you if you keep acting like this."

She just sat there, her big eyes taking in everything I said. I was starting to feel bad. Then I remembered that Lilith was off having a good time with Tad while I was lecturing this chick on blue balling me.

"I need to go," I suddenly said. I was getting mad. I needed my space. "I think you should go back to your friends. Tell my friends I cut out."

"Will you call me?"

I just stared at her. Was she kidding me? Did she think she even had a shot at anything after all was said and done? Was she that dumb? For a college girl, she was quite naïve.

I just grabbed my cigarette pack, found a pen on the dashboard, and handed them to her.

"Write your number on that," I sighed. Her whole face suddenly lit up as she smiled and happily jotted it down. Unbelievable.

I waited for her to climb out of the van and watched her walk back to the club. Too bad. She was cute. I lit my last cigarette from my pack before crumbling the box and tossing it out the window. Then I left.

The memory faded. I was wired and sitting in Freddie's car. A meter maid tapped on the window, bending down to look at me. It was her. I groaned as I rolled down my window.

"Let me sit with you for a spell," she smiled. "You got a long wait, anyway."

I nodded and leaned over to unlock the passenger door. As much as I despised her, I did not mind the company. There was something about her, but I couldn't place it. I didn't know her, but she definitely knew me. There was nothing to hide from her. It was as if she knew the trash I was and welcomed it.

"So," she said after getting in and shutting the door. "You remember anything?"

"What is that?" I asked. "Is this whole memory flashing back time travel bullshit some sort of lesson?"

"It's your life flashing before your eyes," she laughed. "Literally. Not that hard to figure that one out."

Again, I groaned. She waited while I calmed down and rethought the memory.

"Should have never thrown that cigarette pack out," I finally said. "Should have called her. Then maybe she wouldn't have been on this dumbass list."

"Maybe. Not sure. I think that would have made everything worse, though."

"What do you mean?"

"Anything else you remember?" she asked, ignoring my question. "Think hard."

"I don't know. I don't even know what I did to her! I knew her for like thirty minutes. She's lucky she ended up with me that night. I knew to step away. Some other guy might have not been as understanding with her as I was, you know?"

She stared at me with a look of disgust and disbelief on her face.

"Oh, wow. Look at you. Hector Addams, the hero because he didn't rape a girl. Yay," she said, sarcastically.

"That's not…no…stop…" I was flustered. Why is this woman such a pain in my ass? "Who are you, anyway? I don't even know your name."

"Give me one then," she said.

"How about Bitch?"

"Okay. I deserve that," she laughed. "But how about Destiny? Since I am your guide to destiny."

"That's stupid, but whatever," I said. "Are you an angel? Or a—a demon?"

"Angel. Demon. All the same."

The car grew quiet. I took another hit of my coke. She rolled her eyes and shook her head.

"You are just going through the motions, huh?" she finally spoke. "No emotions? No questions? No why is this happening to me?"

"My whole life is just going through the motions," I shrugged. "Learned that early on. Why was I born here? Why was I born with the life of Heck Addams? Why am I going to die? It just is."

"It's sad that you believe that. No deeper levels to your thoughts."

Again, I shrugged. God, this psycho was irritating by turning all therapist on me. I wasn't crazy. I was just me: Hector Addams, born in a shit town trying to live with a shit life. It wasn't that deep.

"Well, you can't sit here all night," she sighed. "You are wasting time."

"I don't know what else to do. I bet you know where she is."

"I do."

"Then why don't you just tell me!"

"I did. It's in your flashback."

"I told you I threw her number out," I reminded her. She was starting to get to me.

"Not that."

I closed my eyes and went over the details of the memory. The music that was playing. Tad. Brenda's preppy clothes. Lilith's keychains. The van. The small talk about our jobs. I towed cars. She was a cashier at—

"Bargains and Deals," I said out loud.

"Bingo," Destiny grinned. "I knew you were a smart cookie."

"What are the chances she still works there?"

"That is for me to know and for you to find out," she laughed, letting herself out of the car. "Good luck."

That was the next step. Bargains and Deals. Not sitting in front of a club waiting for it to open, hoping Brenda would either walk in or someone would know where to find her.

I pulled out of my parking spot and tried not to speed. I couldn't chance being pulled over, between the blow on me and I had no doubt there was a warrant out for my arrest since I disappeared from the hospital. Being arrested would fuck up any chance I had of getting my eternal bliss.

Bargains and Deals was what used to be a five and ten. Now they just sell low-quality products and groceries. It is every addict's favorite store. Buy crappy items and nearly expired lunch meats and save your money for the alcohol and drugs.

The store was a mess with an uninterested security guard at the door. I walked quickly, passing by the aisles for a quick glance. I saw my favorite dark angel no longer wearing the meter maid costume, but the uniform of a store clerk. She was pricing and stocking no-name, dented cans of dog food.

"Is she still working here?" I asked as I approached her. I looked down to see she was wearing a name tag that said "Destiny" on it and rolled my eyes. I knew she was a supernatural being of sorts, but she had a weird sense of humor.

"I thought it was a nice touch," she laughed.

"Whatever. Is she here?"

"Oooh, just because we had a nice chat, doesn't mean I'm on your side," she mocked. "Or am I?"

"Stop with the cryptic shit," I snarled. Angel or devil, I was going to hit her, and I was not sure how smart that would be since she held my fate in her hands.

She smiled. No, she grinned. That evil fucking grin of hers. But her eyes said something different as she glanced down at my clenched hand.

"Always thinking with your fists," she said quietly. I detected softness. Was she breaking down? She sighed, rolled her eyes, and then nodded to the right.

I headed off in search of Brenda once again. I looked up and down all the aisles to the right. I spotted an older gentleman, who was the manager, checking a clipboard, a woman with big hair and snapping gum directing a customer on where to find toilet cleaner, and a tired-looking, very pregnant girl putting up sale signs in the arts and crafts section. Everyone else was a customer.

I started to walk back to Destiny, but something stopped me. Stepping back, I glanced down the aisle that held the glue, glitter, and construction paper. The pregnant girl was clipping a sign to a shelf. I looked at her carefully.

Her light brown hair was pulled back with some curls that escaped, making her look messy. Her face bore no makeup. Just the look of someone who was done with life. She was too young to have that look on her face. Her swollen belly could not be contained by her polo shirt, and she was self-conscious about that. She kept pulling the shirt down every few seconds like a nervous tic. Her eyes were lifeless and dull. No youthful spark. This was a girl just going through the motions of life. This was Brenda Wilson.

This was not the girl I remembered from the club. The bright and bubbly girl who seemed so innocent. This was not the college co-ed who claimed it was her first time out and about clubbing and flirting. As my drunken mother would say, this was a girl who was used up and hung out to dry. And my mother would know because Brenda had the same look about her that my mother had pretty much my entire life.

She must have sensed me standing there because she looked up from her little stack of signs. She just stared at me, recognizing me but not showing any emotion. I had no clue what to say or how to approach her. I did not even know how I hurt her. She was just a random stranger in a random club on a random night. A girl I used to try and make Lilith jealous.

"Heck, right?" she finally spoke.

"Hey. Yeah…Brenda?" I tried to appear friendly and nonchalant. Just a guy shopping for a good deal on synthetic cheese or cheap wrapping paper. Truth be told, if it was not for my little card of names and Destiny herself, I would not even remember Brenda's name. I'm not sure I would even remember that night.

"Look at you!" I continued, fully aware of how awkward and phony I sounded. "You…you're having a baby. Wow!"

She turned red and tugged at the front of her shirt.

We stood there, an uncomfortable silence between us, with stickers, pom-pom balls, and all the other crafts a first grader might need to make a shitty diorama around us. How do I even begin this conversation? How do I maneuver this weirdness between two strangers into a speech about amends and forgiveness?

"You remember me," I blurted out with what I hoped was a friendly smile.

"How could I forget," she shrugged. I detected a catch in her voice. Was she going to cry? I was so confused. "You called me a tease."

Was that it? Was that the god-awful, beg-for-forgiveness bad deed I had done? I called her a name? I have called people way worse. Ask Lilith. She always got the blunt of my viscous name-calling. And she gave it back to me just as good.

"I'm sorry?" I said, not knowing what else to say.

"Not a tease anymore, huh?" she responded, looking down at her belly. There was something so sad and pathetic about Brenda. She reminded me so much of my mother. I wonder if this was how my mother looked when she was pregnant with my brother and me. That poor kid was not going to have a chance.

She began to walk away from me, but I reached out, putting my hand on her shoulder to stop her. I turned her to me.

"Okay. Um, I feel like we need to talk about this," I said to her. "Obviously, I hurt you really bad. I need to hear what you have to say to me. Can you do that? Can you talk with me?"

She looked at me suspiciously. I did not blame her. The last time we went to talk, I came on to her and then dumped her. But she was being a tease. I could not deny that.

She sighed with exhaustion and looked down at her watch.

"I guess I'm due for a smoke break," she said. "Meet me outside in the lot?"

I nodded and watched as she waddled to the front of the store. I breathed a sigh of relief. I did not have her forgiveness yet, but I was so close. What I thought would be the hardest name on my list just got so much easier.

Once outside, I leaned on the hood of Freddie's car and lit up a cigarette. It was only a few minutes before she came out, her winter jacket not closing around her belly. She pulled her pack of smokes from her pocket. It was the trendy, long, skinny cigarettes marketed for women. Lilith would have laughed so hard at that one.

"Should you be smoking?" I asked, motioning to her belly.

"Do you care?" she shot back, her face the epitome of someone who just did not give a shit. I still had a hard time believing this was the same girl from the club.

"Wow, you really changed, huh?" I remarked.

"Well, I was only fifteen," she said. I almost choked on my drag.

"What?" I screeched.

She laughed a little and nodded. Then she became sullen again.

"Yep. Fifteen. I did try and tell you. It was my first time out. My friend's brother got a job at the club, and snuck us in. We got all dressed up and did our best to look older…made up this whole college story…" she trailed off, lost in a memory. Something told me those friends were long gone.

"First time out, first time hanging with boys, first time drinking," she continued.

"First kiss?" I had to know.

She took a drag from her skinny cigarette before flicking it into the parking lot. She looked right at me and nodded.

"I'm sorry that your first kiss wasn't with some popular high school jock named Cory or some shit like that, but you could have gotten me in a whole shitload of trouble!"

I did not mean to yell and instantly regretted it when she flinched. I took a deep breath to try and calm myself. This was not the apology I was supposed to give her. There was something else. I still could not put my finger on it.

"I tried to tell you and you called me a tease," she reminded me. "I didn't know how to play the game and you were my first lesson. Boys don't like teases. Boys won't call you back and take you out and spend time with you if you are a tease."

I was starting to get it. I was beginning to understand how my choice of one little word affected her. Especially since she was only a kid. Her innocence on that night seemed so obvious now. She was not just a typical, flighty flirt. She was just a kid.

"I realized that to keep a guy, you can't tease. Or so I thought," she continued. "More lessons for me, I guess. I would sleep with guys to keep them. But now I am no longer a tease. Instead, I am now…"

"A slut," I said. She was not wrong. Everyone knew that. Girls could not win in the game of sex.

She nodded; her face still blank.

"So, I became a slut," she said. "Only, that didn't keep a guy around. Made other guys interested, though. But they weren't sticking around. Not for long, anyway. Eventually, a girl starts to get desperate to keep a guy."

She looked down at her belly and rubbed it.

"This is my second," she continued. "I have an eighteen-month-old at home. My mom watches him."

"Oh," was all I could say. She was just like my mom. Two kids back-to-back. The dead look on her face. The smoking and not giving a shit how her actions affect her kid.

"My boyfriend—their father—he's hardly around anymore. It'll be over the moment this kid pops out," she admitted. "Babies don't keep them around either."

"You're better off," I told her. "My father stuck around. Did me and my brother no good. He's in prison now. He was always trying to scam a buck. He said it was to feed us and house us, but we rarely saw the money. Now? My mother is a horrible woman. My brother and I are no good."

"Obviously," she muttered.

"Hey, I'm just trying to talk with you. I didn't know you were just a kid. I didn't know you were going to take what some random stranger from a bar said to you so seriously," I said. "And honestly, from the bottom of my heart, I am truly sorry."

"Why?" she laughed. "You said it yourself. You didn't know. I'm the one who lied to you. I'm the one who shouldn't have been there that night. I'm the one who couldn't handle being called a tease and ruined her life. I'm an unwed mom of two, no high school diploma with a dead-end job in a run-down trash store."

"Look…" I paused, trying to collect my thoughts. "Brenda, it's not too late. I am sorry I somehow set you on a path that can affect the next generation. I'm standing here and I can't help but wonder if this is what happened to my mother. Or my grandmother, because lord knows they are both a bitch and a half. But maybe someone spoke one word to them, one wrong word, one unkind word, and now I have to pay for it."

"I don't understand."

"I'm saying, break the cycle. Don't let my being an asshole bring you down. Get rid of the boyfriend. You want to work at keeping a man? Concentrate on your son. Work on keeping him and this baby."

"Nobody's taking my babies!"

"Nobody took me and my brother, but my mother…she never got an ounce of respect from us. She doesn't deserve it either," I said, sadly.

Her eyes narrowed.

"Look, I'm sorry for what I said and how I treated you. And I'm not gonna lie, even if you were of age, I would have said the same bullshit. Men are assholes. I'm an asshole," I said. This was so different from my speech to Heather. I was not acting or spouting half-lies. I was not trying to be inspirational either. There was no love in my words. I was just telling Brenda the truth. Someone needed to.

"Come on," I continued. "Don't let my actions make your kids assholes, too. Don't let me and any other jackass that used you and called you names make you a lesser mother. Rise above us. Prove to us that men can be raised right."

She sighed, jamming her fists into her pockets. She glanced behind me. The manager was waving for her to come back in, motioning that her break was over.

"I gotta go," she said, walking away. "Thanks for the talk."

"I'm sorry!" I called out after her. "Do you forgive me?"

She turned around. No tears. No relief. Just that sullen, tired face. She had the look everyone in Garden Hallows eventually gets. I doubted anything I said to her sunk in. Nothing was going to change. It was too late for her. She shrugged her shoulders.

"I guess."

And with that, she turned back around and disappeared behind the store's automatic doors. She was gone and I was left in the parking lot feeling confused.

Destiny walked out the exit door, a smirk on her face. She unclipped the name tag and tossed it aside into the darkness. I heard it bounce on the concrete with a clink.

"That was some speech you gave her. You had to dig deep down to reach those feelings, huh?" she said, putting a fist over her chest and thumping it. "Straight from the heart, right Heck?"

"Fuck you."

"And there he is! The Heck Addams we all know and love…or hate" she laughed. "Honestly, thought you were getting soft in your dying days."

"Did that count? Was that forgiveness?" I asked. I was still unsure if Brenda's weak answer was a real answer. And I didn't have time for Destiny's bullshit sarcasm.

"Check the list," she shrugged before walking away from me.

I dug the card out of my pocket and read it. Her name was gone. Three names remained.

Julia Collins
Melissa Bracco
Lilith Patton

IV.

I arrived home to the same scene that has been going on in my house for years. A messy living room, a sloppy mother, a highly annoyed brother because I took his car, and my own exhausted mind spinning out of control. I headed straight to the kitchen to rummage around for something to eat while Freddie yelled at me, and my mother yelled even louder for him to shut up so she could hear her show.

I found some old leftover pizza in the fridge and nuked it for a few seconds just to kill the bacteria. Eating healthy was not a thing in our house, but old questionable food for meals was. Freddie and I had been pretty much fending for ourselves since we were kids.

I grabbed the slice and a bottle of beer and sat down in the living room in the only chair that was not piled with a towering mess of laundry, newspapers, and fast-food wrappers. My mother was sprawled on the couch as usual. A glass of her chosen spirit of the day in her hand, a cigarette between her fingers, and an ashtray balanced ever so carefully on her belly.

I stared at her, trying to remember a time when she was youthful and full of life. I tried to remember a time she made an ounce of effort toward me or Freddie. I could not remember a home-cooked meal or some encouraging words. Maybe there was a faded glimpse or two of her joking and laughing when I was very young, but for the most part I just always remembered being a bother. A pain in the ass brat. And she was always ragged looking. Tired and dead in the eyes just like Brenda.

"What?" she said, noticing me staring at her.

"Nothing," I replied, shaking my head.

"You got something to say? You want to start?"

"Jesus Christ, Ma!" I yelled. "Not everything has to be a fight with you. I was just looking at you and wondering…"

"Wondering what?" She sat up, slamming her glass on the coffee table. I could not even look at my mother without her going into defense mode.

"God, you really are such a bitch," I muttered, throwing my pizza crust at her.

"Fuck you! I'm just laying here trying to watch my shows and you come and treat me like this?!"

"Oh, my God! I wasn't doing anything! You are a crazy psycho!" I stood up and grabbed my smokes. I needed air. "Have another drink, Annie!"

I stormed out into the yard. Even though I was seething, I could hear that she was already over it. She was laughing along with some lame laugh track for some lame sitcom. I lit up my cigarette and looked up.

Julia Collins was next on my list, and I had a feeling she would be easy enough to take off the list. She was the girl next door, and I could see her bedroom window from my yard. I realized it had been a while since I had seen her, though. There was once a time when I looked up at her house, I would see her standing there, just staring at me.

Julia was creepy. She was a couple of years younger than me, always over-eager, trying too hard, and she was fat. She was a pig.

And it was well known that Julia Collins had a crush on me.

I decided to take care of Julia in the morning. I was hitting that wall where I either needed sleep or speed to keep going. Sleep sounded pretty fucking good. My body was still healing from the accident. My mind needed to slow down. It was easier to just shut down and turn off all the memories, emotions, and the thought of my impending death. I would deal with it all in the morning. That was the story of my life: deal with it later. Sometimes, I didn't deal with it at all.

I shut down as soon as I flopped on my bed. I spiraled into that dark blackness that comes with too much drinking and drugging. It was a place that was empty of all feelings. No happiness. No sadness. No jealousy. No anger. Just a feeling of barely existing. I welcomed it. If death was anything like this bleak, almost comforting nothingness, maybe it won't be so bad.

I woke up in the morning to my mother pounding on the door and yelling at me. I cursed under my breath as I tried to blink the sleep out of my eyes. The screaming did not stop, and my head was not fully clear from the dark fog. I couldn't comprehend what her problem was.

I yanked on my jeans and swung my door open. She was mid-pound and almost hit me.

"Why aren't you at work?" she screamed, her breath reeking of Jack Daniels and cigarettes. I detected vomit too, which meant she went to town last night without ever leaving her couch.

"What? Why do you care?"

"That fuckin' phone has been ringing all goddamn morning and your boss must have left a million messages on the machine!"

As if on cue, the phone rang again. I walked past my mother and gave her a little shove with my shoulder. I picked up the phone in the kitchen. It was my boss.

"You're late," was the first thing he said to me. Honestly, my boss was a halfway decent guy. He put up with a lot of my shit over the last couple of years. I should have been fired on day one.

"No shit," was my response. I didn't even know what time it was. I glanced at the kitchen clock to see it was approaching eleven in the morning. I remembered that today was the day I needed to approach Julia. Good old fat cow next door Julia. And then I remembered my job did not mean shit to me anymore. What was once an easy way to make some bucks to score some highs and maybe pay a bill or two was now a thing of the past. I was going to be dead in a matter of days. Fuck my nice boss and fuck my job.

"Yeah, I'm not coming in. I quit."

And with that, I hung up. It was really that simple.

"What the fuck, Heck?!" my mother yelled. "You better have another job lined up. I'm not having no dead-beat son of mine living here!"

"Takes a dead-beat to raise a dead-beat," I grumbled.

"You are just like your father. No good criminal."

"Don't worry. I'm outta here by Saturday night, okay?" I was not lying. It was true. According to Destiny, I would be dead by the stroke of midnight.

I wondered how it would happen. Would I just drop? Would I fall asleep and never wake up? Maybe a heart attack or stroke. Whatever it was, I would not mind doing it right in front of my mother. Let her live with that image for the rest of her life; her son just dropping right before her eyes. I hoped she would be grief-stricken and overwhelmed with guilt.

I watched as she opened the fridge and pulled out her tomato juice. That, she always made sure we had stocked in the house. All the ingredients for a good Bloody Mary in the morning and whatever spirits and mixed drinks that moved her throughout the rest of the day.

"Yeah, you don't want to be late for Jenny Jones or whatever fuckin' talk show is coming on now," I laughed, walking out.

I needed a shower. If I was going to approach Julia, I should at least be presentable. Give her something to remember me by.

I looked in the mirror as the hot water warmed up. My bruises were starting to turn yellowish. I lightly fingered my stitched lip. It was not too bad. If I didn't shave, the threads blended a little. I looked like hell. Barely twenty-three years old and I already looked like hell. They are not lying when they say partying ages you.

I stepped into the hot shower and just stood there, letting it rain down my head, shoulders, and back, easing all the tension. My mind started to get fuzzy, and I knew what was coming next—a memory.

We had just returned from a day at the beach. I was not a beach person, but it was Lilith's idea to get out of the neighborhood for the day, head down to the lake, and shake things up. With Mitch, Freddie, Heather, and some other random people we occasionally hung out with, we piled into her van. A cooler of beer and a bag of weed at the beach made for a fun day.

By the time we came home, we did not want the fun to end. We continued the party in my yard. It was simple. People sitting around on old beat-up patio furniture, good music on the boom box, a joint being passed, and some of my mother's liquor was brought out.

I was feeling good as Lilith was putting some aloe on my burned shoulders, massaging it when Julia came around the corner of my yard. Waddled was more like it. Her white shorts were all bunched up, caught in the friction on her jelly thighs. Her red shirt was a crop top, and no one needed to see her pale blubber belly ballooning out. She had on an overwhelming amount of blue eye shadow and her hair was sprayed and teased into a style that went out with the turn of the decade. Did she think she looked good? Did she even own a mirror?

She was carrying a tray with a pitcher of what looked like lemonade and a plate of cookies. Her face was beaming but nervous.

She was always staring and waving at me whenever she saw me, but this was the closest she ever came. It was weird.

"What the fuck…" I muttered with a snicker under my breath as Lilith shushed me. We all stopped talking and stared at Julia. She stood there, awkwardly holding her tray and shifting her weight from one foot to the other. I wondered if it was because her feet could not handle her weight or if she had to pee.

"Hi there," Lilith finally spoke up, her voice friendly. I sighed in disgust. Why did Lilith have to say anything? Julia was like a stray cat. If we ignored her, she would go away.

"Hi!" Julia squeaked out. Her face turned up into a huge smile. She just lit up at Lilith noticing her. "I'm Julia. I live next door and saw Hector had some friends over and…well…I baked some cookies today and I thought maybe you might want some?"

"Nah, we're good," I said as Lilith slapped me on the back of my head.

"Speak for yourself, Dick," Mitch chimed in, reaching over to Julia's tray and grabbing a cookie.

"Sit down," Lilith encouraged. "Come hang out."

I knew Lilith was doing this on purpose. She knew that Julia had her weird little crush on me. Lilith was doing this for her own entertainment to see where this would go. She was spiteful like that.

We all watched as she put the tray down on the table among the empty cans and bottles and filled ashtrays. She lowered herself onto a lawn chair and I could see the thin aluminum legs just screaming for relief from her weight.

"Aren't you going to introduce everyone, Heck?" Lilith said. She was smiling, but I knew Lilith well. As well as myself. Her smile was not a friendly one.

"Julia…" I grumbled. "You know my brother, Freddie. And that's Heather, Mitch…friends from around town."

"And I know your girlfriend, Lilith," Julia giggled.

Lilith burst out laughing, almost choking on the beer she was drinking. Julia frowned.

"Sorry," Lilith said, continuing to laugh. "I'm not his girlfriend."

"Oh," Julia exclaimed, and I could see her face light up with hope. I groaned and threw a look at Lilith. We should have just let Julia believe Lilith and I were a thing.

"But you two are always together," Julia continued. "I always see you guys. You pick him up and drive him to work sometimes, and you are always here, or he is always leaving with you."

"What do you do?" I asked her. "Just stand at your window and spy on me?"

Again, Lilith smacked the back of my head. That was getting annoying. Julia, in the meantime, turned several shades of pink and began giggling like a fool.

"Nooo," she said. "I just noticed, that's all. How come you guys aren't boyfriend and girlfriend"

"Yeah, how come?" Freddie quipped. I fired him a look. This was getting out of control.

"Because there is no way in hell I am dating this asshole," Lilith laughed. Now it was her turn to get a look from me. When did I become the brunt of everyone's joke?

"Oh really," I said to Lilith. "You want to fuckin' go there? There is no way in hell I would ever date you, bitch."

Lilith laughed even harder.

"You couldn't handle me anyway," she said. "I'm the only one that's not afraid of you and gives it right back to you."

She was right about that. Every girl I was with always ended up afraid of my temper. Not Lilith. Her temper matched mine.

"Oh, Hector's not that bad," Julia chimed. "I bet with the right girlfriend, he's a real sweetie."

Lilith's face suddenly changed. She went from laughing to staring at Julia with curiosity. I could see the wheels turning in Lilith's head.

She was ready to up her game. She was ready to be entertained.

"The right girlfriend, huh?" Lilith said. "And what would the right girlfriend for Hector be?"

"I don't know…cooks and cleans for him? Doesn't always tease him? See that he's hardworking and handsome and sometimes, when his mother is yelling at him, just tell him to come over, and keep him calm and let him know it's okay…" she trailed off, realizing everyone was just staring at her with disbelief. Her pink face was now crossing into red.

"So…you," Lilith said softly, her grin bigger than ever. She placed her hand on my shoulder and squeezed. "You, *Julia*, are the right girlfriend for good old Hector Addams."

Lilith chuckled. She was entertained, but she was not done yet. I could feel it coming like a bad punchline to a bad joke. Everyone but Julia knew what was coming. Poor, awkward, fat, weird Julia. It was her fault. She should have kept herself on the other side of the hedges, watching from her creepy distance.

"Hear that, Hector," Lilith drawled, reaching out and cradling my face in her hand. "Julia is the perfect girl for you. She'll keep this handsome face safe and loved. Not like me. Right?"

"Lilith, shut the fuck up. Don't start," I muttered, slapping her hand away.

"I'm not good enough for you. But apparently, Julia is," she continued, her voice teasing. "Are you good enough for Julia? Think she can handle you like me?"

Julia squirmed in her chair. She was no longer smiling and beaming. Her eyes darted around to avoid looking at me or anyone. My blood was raging. I could hear it in my ears. My fists clenched. Lilith saw that and grinned. Only Lilith would purposefully get me like this. I stared at Julia, breathing heavily. Who the fuck invited her?

"I-I—" she stammered.

"Oh, shut the fuck up, you fat fuck!" I screamed, standing up suddenly. She flinched and gasped. Her chin began to quiver.

"Heck, no," Lilith said softly. She suddenly had a different tone. She got what she wanted. Now she was going to play the nice guy and act all innocent.

"And you!" I yelled, grabbing Lilith and pulling her to her feet. It did not surprise me to hear my friends groan. They all have seen this shit show before. They did not even bother to get in between Lilith and me.

"What? What the fuck you gonna do? Huh?" Lilith screamed back, shoving at me. "You are such a dickwad!"

More screaming ensued. It was a typical night. She slapped me on the chest. I shoved her just a little. She slammed her foot on my toes. I grabbed her and shook her. There was a ton of name-calling and cursing. Lilith and I both had an extensive and imaginative vocabulary when it came to that. It ended as it almost always did; me on my knees because Lilith resorted to kicking me in the balls before storming off down my driveway.

I let out a blood-curdling scream and tried to catch my breath as the pain subsided. Looking up, I could see Julia was still sitting there looking scared out of her mind. I pulled myself up and picked up her stupid tray and flung it over the hedges to her yard. We could all hear it crash and shatter on the Collins' cement patio.

"Real nice!" I heard Lilith shout from the front yard.

"Why are you even still fuckin' here?!" I screamed, unsure if I meant that to be for Julia or Lilith. Both of them needed to go.

I stormed to the front yard in time to see Lilith climbing into her van. I picked up an empty wine bottle from the pile of garbage on the side of my house and flung it at the van while screaming a primal noise from the back of my throat.

"Go to hell!" I screamed as she pulled out from in front of my house.

"I will!" she yelled back with a laugh. "And I'll take you with me!"

With that, she was gone. I turned around to see Julia standing there, trying to quietly sneak past me and get back to the safety of her own home.

"Go on, you fat pig! Go cry wee wee wee all the way home, you little fuckin' piggy!"

That broke her. A sob escaped from her mouth, and she ran with every ounce of her being, jiggling into her house.

The shower started to turn cold when my mind cleared from the fog. I turned the water off and grabbed a towel. The memory did not make me feel that bad. It was her fault. No one made her fat. No one invited her to sit at my house. She had watched and stalked me enough times to know that my house was a den of toxicity. She had asked for it.

The sad thing was that Lilith and I were perfectly fine the next day. While Julia was probably crying and cramming cookies and ice cream down her gullet, Lilith and I had gotten over it. We were still best friends.

I would still see Julia from time to time. I did not want to encourage her to ever invite herself into my life again, so I made her miserable. I would oink or moo anytime she was around. It worked. She never approached me again. She would still lurk in her windows though, still watching. Eventually, I stopped noticing her.

I sighed, getting dressed. Might as well get it over with. I ran through the whole "making amends" speech in my head. I would have to blame alcoholism and drug addiction for being such a mean bully to her. It would work. Fat girls have no self-esteem.

I walked next door and rang her doorbell. It was not long until Mrs. Collins answered it. She squinted at me in a way that made it known she did not like me. Who could blame her? My family was the symbol of white trash. My house was run down and unkempt. Barren lawn in some spots, overgrown weeds in others. We had no shame in the number of alcohol bottles and cans that went out with the trash, if the trash even made it to the curb that day. There was no shame in our behavior either. The yelling and screaming and loud music would go on for all hours of the night.

The Collins' house was simple and neat. The lawn always trimmed, colorful and seasonal flowers in the flower boxes. Quiet. Their house was heaven to our hell.

But still, I persisted despite Mrs. Collins' judgmental stare. I put on my best smile which I then realized probably made me look deranged with my bruises and stitched lip.

"Hey, Mrs. Collins," I greeted after clearing my throat.

She did not respond. Just glared.

"I was wondering if Julia happened to be around?"

Her glare turned into a look of disbelief. It was the look that screamed, "How Dare You!" If she was wearing pearls, she would be clutching them.

"What do you want with my Julia?" she said with a low growl in her tone. I took an involuntary step back.

"Nothing, really," I tried to charm. "Just haven't seen her in a while. Thought I'd do the neighborly thing and say hello. Check up on her."

"I don't think so."

The door slammed shut. No explanation. Not that one was needed. She, no doubt, heard the hundreds of times I made farm animal noises at her daughter. Maybe if she raised her with proper eating habits…

I could not let myself go there, being the product of a mother who did not check to see if I ate at all. I could do nothing but shake my head and walk away from the Collins' house before she called the cops on me. It would not be the first time a neighbor of ours called the cops on us. Shit, my own family even called the cops on each other.

Speaking of stellar mothers, mine was still awake, drinking her afternoon lunch and watching two people accuse each other of cheating while sitting on some cheap-looking stage with a talk show host trying, unsuccessfully, to diffuse the situation.

"I saw you at the Collins'," she said, not taking her eyes off the television. "Whatcha want with them?"

"Looking for Julia." I started to walk to my room to rethink how I was going to find her. As usual, I had no time for my mother's bullshit.

"She ain't around much no more," my mother began. "Not since she started college."

I stopped in my tracks. It never occurred to me that my mother was aware of the outside world other than her television and booze.

"Oh yeah?" I said, walking back. I had to tread lightly. One wrong word could set my mother off on another tangent of fuck yous. "I didn't know she went to college."

"Yep. Little Miss Smarty Pants hightailed it to Newton East U. Heard her mother bragging about a scholarship."

"Probably needed to get away from Mrs. Collins' clutches," I joked.

My mother side-eyed me and chuckled.

"Yeah, she's a bitch."

That was the extent of the conversation. She was back to watching her show, cigarette in one hand and glass of something brown and potent in the other. I guess she moved on from her morning Bloody Mary.

But that was all I needed. Julia was at school. Newton East University to be exact. She must have been dorming there because it was just over an hour's drive away and I had not seen her in a while. All I had to do was find her on campus.

I quietly opened Freddie's bedroom door and reached in for his car keys on top of the dresser. I did not care if it pissed him off.

After Saturday, he would never have to worry about me taking his car again. I wondered how long it would be before Freddie started rummaging through my shit to take after I died. I knew my mother and he would be looking for anything they could get. They were going to pawn off everything I owned as soon as my body hit the ground. I did not feel guilty about taking his car again.

With nothing but a lighter and a pack of smokes, I hit the road. I blasted the local hard rock radio station, my fingers drumming on the steering wheel as I sped down the highway. There was hardly any traffic, so I made it to Newton East University Campus in no time.

The campus was not a big one, but I still had no clue where anything was. I grabbed an empty parking spot in one of their few lots and began walking. There was a map posted and I took a look. It was disheartening to see the campus had four dorms. I started to head to one of them.

As I passed people on the walkways, I would stop them. I tried my best to look casual and friendly, but I knew I stood out like a sore thumb with my long hair, ripped jeans, leather jacket, and dirty work boots.

"Hey," I would greet them. "Do you know where I can find Julia Collins? No? Okay, thanks."

I would say I was her cousin if anyone looked at me like I was a serial killer or something. People shook their heads and scurried away.

"We up to Julia already?" a girl's voice teased from behind me. I stopped walking and looked up to the sky with a long sigh. I did not even have to look. It was her. Destiny.

She was dressed like a typical college co-ed: tights, a plaid skirt, and a sweater. She wore a thick headband in her dark curly hair. She had on a pair of glasses that she and I both knew she did not need.

"Destiny," I said. I could not help but think that she was looking hot. Too bad she was a bitch from hell.

She smiled as if she could read my mind. For some reason, I felt my cheeks get hot and turn red. That was an odd feeling for me. I hardly ever blushed.

"So," she said, looping her arm in mine. "You are looking for Julia Collins. No luck? What's your plan? How are you going to find one little girl on a great big campus?"

"*Little*," I snickered. "I'll find her! Just gonna hit the dorms."

"And what? Knock on every door? No. That won't work. Should I help you?"

She looked up at me, grinning that bitchy grin. I stopped walking and stared down at her, my jaw clenching.

"Stop playing fuckin' games with me," I growled.

"Oh, but you love it! Gets your blood going. Makes you feel good," she practically purred.

"Either help me or don't. But stop teasing me."

She pouted at me, her bottom lip jutting out dramatically. It was sexy. Again, her eyebrow raised, and I blushed. I pushed her away from me.

"What the fuck?" I mumbled.

"Okay. Fine, Hector," she giggled. "I'll help you. You need to stop shoving girls around though. One day you are going to push the wrong girl. Maybe you already did."

Shit. What did she mean by that? Did I just seal my fate to hell by pushing her? It wasn't even a real shove. Just a playful push of annoyance.

"Hartley Dorm," she sighed. Her mood changed. She suddenly seemed bored. "Go on. Get it over with."

"Thanks," I smiled. I walked away to find another map to check where Hartley Dorm was. I lit a cigarette to smoke on my walk. Destiny was already long gone. She disappeared in a blink.

There was a lone desk with a volunteer student sitting there in the vestibule of the dorm, reading a book. She nodded to me and pointed to a notebook for me to sign in.

"Do you know what room I can find my cousin in? Julia Collins?"

"3G," she replied without even taking her eyes up from the book. The whole security thing was a weak formality.

I found a staircase and climbed to the third floor. I was breathing hard and needed to stop and take a break when I got to the top. This was a first. If I was not going to be dead in two days, I would have had to slow the smoking down.

Or maybe it was not the smoking, but my impending death itself. Was this the beginning? Was I starting to succumb to whatever awaited me on Saturday? Was this going to be a slow and painful death? I wouldn't put it past Destiny to do that. She liked to tease and play with me like a cat with a mouse.

My breathing regulated again, and I walked down the hall. 3G. It stood before me, adorned in little magazine cut-outs of bands, an inspirational quote, and a dry-erase board to leave a message.

I knocked. It was only a few quick seconds before the door opened. A short, petite girl answered. She was freckled with short red hair, round wire-framed glasses, and wore a baggy black dress with combat boots. She was what Lilith would have called "New Age."

"Hi. Is Julia around?" I asked.

She stared at me like she knew me, but just could not put her finger on where she knew me from. Then, her eyes grew wide behind her glasses.

"You're Hector, right?" she asked. "Heck Addams?"

Now it was my turn to make my eyes wide. Did I know her?

"Sorry," she laughed. "Come in. I'm Julia's roommate. Colleen."

I walked in, still confused by how she knew me. The room was empty. Julia was nowhere to be seen. The room was small with two of everything: narrow beds, desks, chairs, and dressers. A window and a small fridge were between the two beds.

One-half of the room was messy and plastered with what I

assumed were literary quotes and bands like Depeche Mode, The Cure, and U2. The other half was tidy. On the wall next to the bed was a mishmash collage of photographs. No wonder this little emo elf knew who I was. All the photos were of me.

"What the actual fuck?" I said to no one in particular.

"I know! Creepy, right?" Colleen laughed.

"No shit."

I walked closer to examine the photos. They were all from the viewpoint of Julia's house. There were several of me getting in or out of my car. Taking out the trash. Being picked up by friends. Making a deal with my weed or coke dealer. Smoking a cigarette in my yard. One of me was shirtless in my bedroom. Several of me with Lilith. Laughing with Lilith. Fighting with Lilith. Just chilling with Lilith.

"Yeah, she's obsessed with you," Colleen said. "I have a request in to get a new roommate next semester."

"Holy crap," I said. "I knew it was bad, but I didn't know it was this bad."

"It is so weird. Between this and her eating habits…" Colleen trailed off. "Anyway, she should be back any minute. Her photog class ended like fifteen minutes ago."

"Photog? Good to know she put her bullshit camera sessions to good use."

"I don't know why you are here. Didn't think you even knew she existed but go easy on her. She's…fragile."

"There ain't nothing fragile about that heifer," I mumbled.

"What was that?" she asked, sounding confused.

Before I could repeat myself, the door opened. A thin, pretty blond girl walked in. She carried a duffel bag and wore tight workout clothes under a bright pink windbreaker. Her hair was pulled up in a high ponytail.

She gasped when she saw me and took a step back. All the color drained from her face. I was even more confused. Just how popular was I in Julia's little circle?

"Hector?"

Her voice was so familiar. All at once, I could see her. This was the face under the chubby cheeks that squished her eyes.

"Julia?" It was my turn to gasp.

"Okay, looks like you two have some catching up to do. I'm out of here," Colleen quipped. She grabbed an old, beat-up army jacket and a backpack and left quickly, leaving Julia's embarrassment and my awkwardness hanging in the air.

"Why are you here?"

"Um, wait. What the hell is that?" I asked, pointing to the wall of me. "And what the hell happened to you? Because you look fuckin' fantastic."

It was true. She was hot.

She turned bright red and made this weird half-laughing, half-crying noise in the back of her throat. She smiled as her eyes welled up.

"Thank you," she whispered.

"I think you have some explaining to do," I said. I completely ignored the fact that I also had explaining to do. I was aware that her walking into her dorm room with me standing there was just as bizarre as her stalker photos.

"I-I..." and then she began to cry. Sob was more like it. She was like a little kid that got caught with their hand in the cookie jar. She dropped her duffel bag and sat on her bed, her head in her hands, bawling. I felt bad. Kind of. I rolled my eyes before sitting next to her and putting my arm around her.

"Don't cry," I told her. "I didn't mean to make you cry."

"This is just so embarrassing!"

"Well, maybe. I mean, yeah. It's totally fuckin' weird, but maybe you want to explain it to me?"

She tried to catch her breath and nodded. With the back of her jacket sleeve, she wiped her face. I waited, patiently. I had to play this right. I needed her forgiveness, the whole reason I was there, to begin with. I could not scare her off. Colleen was right. Julia was fragile and a mental headcase to boot.

"You know how some girls have these crushes of…of Luke Perry or-or Axl Rose?" she began. I nodded. "Well, I never had that. My childhood crush was always the boy next door. But I didn't have pinups and posters to put on my wall. Instead, I took pictures of you and put them up on my wall."

"But still?" I asked. "I mean, after everything I said to you over the years? After you lost all the weight? Surely, guys hit on you and ask you out. Don't you date? Fool around? Move on from your childhood crush?"

"Yeah. I date. I have fun, but still…"

She trailed off and looked up at me. Her blue eyes were vivid and stunning from the crying.

"You were horrible to me, Hector. But I took that and pretended you were telling me those things because you wanted me to be better for you. That if I lost weight and exercised that you would see the real me. So, I started exercising and watching what I ate. I major in nutrition now and I work out at the gym at least three times a day."

"Wow," was all I could say.

"You are the reason I lost all the weight. I had this whole plan that one day, you would see me at home, and you would see how good I looked," she said. "And you would come over and look at me like you looked at other girls, like Lilith."

I groaned. She still did not get it. Lilith and I were never like that.

"Anyway, I thought you would be all nice to me and realize that you were in love with me…and then I was going to tell you to go to hell."

"Okay. That's twisted, but way to stay committed to a plan for revenge, huh?" I joked. I pushed a strand of her hair that escaped her ponytail out of her face. She seemed to shudder at my touch, and I don't think it was because I repulsed her.

"I'm sorry," she said quietly. "I know this all sounds so stupid."

"No. Weird, yes. But not stupid."

"My therapist says I need to let go of my obsessive behavior."

"Oh, good. You're seeing a therapist. That's good."

I didn't know what else to say with that information.

"She also said I needed closure from you. She suggested burning your pictures, but I just wasn't ready for that."

"I can see that," I chuckled. "But closure is good. I need closure too. I need to make amends for all the horrible things I said to you. It wasn't right. I didn't know what I was doing. I was always half out of my head…drinking…partying…"

"That's okay."

She moved closer to me. I could smell her perfume. It was girly and innocent, like baby powder.

"Do you forgive me? I need you to forgive me," I urged, making my arm a little tighter around her, staring down at her. I could feel the tension between us. I knew what was going to happen and I was going to let it happen. I had two reasons I was going to let it happen: she was hot, and I was dying. It was perfectly reasonable to me.

"You don't even need to ask," she smiled. "You set me on the right track. You were the only one who was truthful with me. If it wasn't for you, I wouldn't look like this now. I needed you."

This girl was actually turning my abusive self into her savior. She needed more than therapy. I could not believe my ears.

I smiled at her because there was no way I was going to argue with her and point out that I was a douchebag if she removed her rose-colored glasses. I gently put my hand under her chin and brought my busted lips to her soft pout. She responded with an excited gasp and instantly threw her arms around my neck.

It only took seconds before I was helping her remove her windbreaker and workout clothes. Her hands fumbled with my belt and jeans. I could almost hear Destiny "tsk-tsking" in my head as I lay down on top of Julia.

I knew I was wasting precious time and the clock was ticking. But I needed this. I could not explain this sudden urge to be held and touched. This was most likely the last time I was ever going to experience physical intimacy and I was not going to die without grabbing this opportunity.

It was nice. Julia seemed unsure of the whole sex thing, but she got the job done. I rolled off of her and she squeezed herself between me and the wall, her head resting on my chest. I could see this bright, beaming smile on her face. Now and then she let out a little giggle. She was proud of herself. She conquered her great white whale. She bedded Hector Addams, the boy next door.

I slowly drifted off, falling into a deep sleep. Somewhere in the hazy distance, I could feel that Julia also fell into a breathing pace akin to a deep slumber. There were no dreams for me. No memories. Just a blissful sleep throughout the night.

I woke up with the morning sun shining through the one window and Colleen fussing around with some books and a bag. I sat up, pulling the sheets around my waist. Julia was still beside me on the bed, smiling and gazing at me with her sleepy blue eyes.

I lit a cigarette as Julia reached out and rubbed my bare back. Colleen scowled at us before grabbing her coat and walking out of the room. She did not seem so happy about me crashing there for the night.

"So," Julia began, sitting up. "I was going to go for a run. You should come with me. It will be fun."

Did she think we were a thing now?

"And then after, if you want, we can grab some breakfast in the cafeteria. I don't eat much, but I bet you're hungry. Or I know this great little coffee shop off campus. We can drive over there?"

I was starving, but there was no way in Destiny's hell I was going out to breakfast with Julia. I had things to take care of. I still had two more names on my list, and I only had until the next day at midnight to do it.

I had to play this carefully. If I made her sad or angry in any way, would that make her forgiveness from the night before null and void?

I looked over my shoulder at her, her face so filled with hope, and dare I say it…love? No, it wasn't love. Just schoolgirl infatuation. This chick needed to grow up.

"Look, Julia…" I said, trying to find the right words to let her down easily. As usual, the right words were always a lie. "I came here for a very specific reason, and it wasn't to fuck you."

The smile fell from her face. Her brows knitted together.

"I…well…I'm dying."

That wasn't a lie. She just didn't need to know the whole Destiny and heaven versus hell crazy crap.

"Dying?" Now her face was one of shock and concern.

"I was in a car accident the other day and while I was there, they ran the standard tests, and they came back that I am dying. I'm not going to be around much longer."

"Cancer?" she squeaked. "What kind? Oh, Hector!"

Oh Lord, she was crying. As much as I was cringing inside, I reached out to her and put my arm around her to comfort her.

"Not cancer," I admitted. "I just wrecked my body with all the drinking and partying. The blow, the pills, the smoking…"

"Wait," she sniffled and wiped her nose. "You can quit. I can help you get better! I can meal plan for you and help you eat properly. There are so many foods with enrichments and vitamins that will rebuild your body! I can do this for you. I'll be there every step of the way."

"No, Julia," I shook my head, removing my arm from her. "It's too late."

"But this is what I do! This is what I major in!" she insisted as I stood up to pull on my jeans. I needed to get away from her. She was a whole new kind of crazy for me.

"Maybe I don't want to stop my ways," I told her, pulling my shirt on. "Besides, I don't have much time. I came here to tell you that I regret all the times I tormented you. And I have more people I need to reach out to. I am not a nice guy. I am horrible, and I've treated people horribly."

"But, Hector—"

"Julia, please," I cut her off. "Last night was amazing. You are an amazing and beautiful girl. You need to take these pictures of me down, and you need to move on. Closure, remember? Let last night be our closure."

She looked at the wall. Her creepy, obsessive wall of me. She reached out and fingered one of the pictures. It had Lilith in it.

"Is Lilith one of the ones you need to see?" she asked. I could hear the jealousy in her voice.

"You do know that Lilith and I were never anything more than friends, right? I mean, you are aware that a guy and girl can be just friends?"

She shook her head.

"No. You guys are more. Look at her face in these pictures. Look at how she looks at you."

"We were just friends," I grumbled, throwing my jacket. "Not anymore, though. I haven't spoken to Lilith in months. Almost a year. So, yeah, Lilith is one of the people I need to see before I die."

She kept looking at the pictures. She could not look at me. I could see her shoulders shaking as she tried so hard to stifle her cries. This girl thought we were going to wake up after a one-night stand and be all rainbows, sunshine, and butterflies. I did not doubt if her crazy ass went to sleep dreaming of weddings and kids and a little house with a white picket fence.

There was nothing left for me to say. I opened my mouth to say good-bye, but I could not even say that. She looked so pathetic, just staring at the wall, naked and wrapped in her nest of sheets and blankets. I had no doubt Colleen was going to have to call someone to come and get her. I imagined Julia would be committed after this.

I left her to wallow in her insanity. My job was done. I not only apologized for all my abusive name-calling, but quite frankly, I made her childhood dreams come true. Not many girls get a night in bed with their crush.

The air was cold as I made my way across the campus and back to Freddie's car. There was a ticket on the windshield, but I just tossed it. It was Freddie's problem, not mine. And by the time he found out about it, I would be long gone.

I cranked up the heat and turned on the radio. Poison's "Unskinny Bop" came blaring on the speakers. I pulled out the card. Only two names remained. Melissa Bracco and Lilith Patton.

V.

Melissa Bracco was an easy find. I knew where she lived, but she was going to be hard to get compassion from. Our relationship was one big nightmare. It was filled with nothing but screaming and fighting. I was not even sure how we ended up together in the first place.

I headed to Melissa's mother's house. That is where she has been living ever since we broke up. There was a ton of morning traffic on the interstate, so it was taking longer than usual to get back to Garden Hollows, away from the university.

I never even thought of Julia again. She was already a distant memory. Just another fuck in the night.

I drummed my fingers on the steering wheel, wishing I had something to wake me up. And not coffee. Something illegal. I could feel the fog beginning to come on as traffic slowly inched forward. I was being drifted into another memory. I didn't want to drift into any memory of Melissa. She was a waste of my time, money, energy, and space.

Melissa Bracco was the only girl I officially lived with, outside of my mother's house. For some insane reason, Melissa and I thought it would be a great idea to get a place of our own. I think it was because we were both cheaters, though neither of us would admit it, and we thought that by living together we could keep a closer eye on each other. It was a relationship built on instability and toxic distrust.

Where we lived was not much. Actually, it was not anything at all. It was a cheap, run-down roadside motel. It lost most of its legit business to the ever-growing corporate hotels that were popping up at the interstate exit. There was no exercise room or free breakfast at this place. Most of the occupants at the motel were people down on their luck or homeless. Those that were fly-by-nights were just that. Some drug addicts looking for a place to shoot up in peace, underage teens looking for a place to drink and party with friends, and the occasional hookers with their johns.

We lived there because, between Melissa's little cashier job at a local hole-in-the-wall video store and my towing job, we couldn't afford anything else. We tried living at my mom's, but Melissa couldn't ignore my mother's abuse like Heather could. Melissa and my mother came to screeching arguments one too many times.

That was Melissa. Always screeching like a feral cat with their claws out and eyes wild. But Melissa was sexy as hell. She was tall and had long, light red hair down to her waist with a few angled wisps framing her face. She loved to wear dark eyeliner with wings on the edges, making her blue eyes seem more like a teal shade. And she was a beast in bed. Maybe because it all always happened after going a round or two of fighting.

It was an unseasonably warm spring night, and I was lying in one of the two motel beds with the television on. Arsenio Hall was introducing his first guest, but I was not paying attention. I was fuming. Melissa was supposed to be home from her shift at the video store over an hour ago.

I heard a knock at the door and peeked out from the tattered and stained curtain. Lilith was standing there, lighting up a smoke. I let her in, flopping back down on the bed.

"I have to make a drop," Lilith announced, walking into the room and taking a seat at the little café table all the rooms were provided with. "Want to come with me? We could hit the bar after. My treat."

I shook my head. I needed to be home for when Melissa came home. I needed to let Melissa know I was not happy. As usual.

"You know…" Lilith said, a grin creeping up on her face. "I know you are pissed right now. She told you she was coming home right after work?"

She knew. Lilith always knew.

"I was actually at the bar before I headed over here," she continued. "She's there. Melissa is there now, with that Greg dude."

I shot up, nostrils flaring.

"Are you fuckin' with me?" I asked. Greg was Melissa's manager. He had his eye on Melissa and was always flirting with her. Melissa knew I couldn't stand him. I did not want her around him outside of work.

"Would I lie to you? I don't lie about shit like Melissa. You know that."

"Fuck!" I screamed.

"Oh, calm down," she laughed. "Clean up and come out with me. Have a good time with me. Show her you don't give a shit."

"Lilith, no. Fuck no!"

"Come on," she sang out. "Why should you wallow in your misery while she's out having a good time doing God knows what with God knows who? We don't have to hit the bar. We can just cruise around, pick up some good shit, and listen to good music."

That did sound good.

"Let Melissa come home and wonder where the fuck you are for once," Lilith went on. "Fuck her."

I nodded. Lilith was right. I needed to get out. I would deal with Melissa when I got back. Maybe even end up at the bar and drag her skinny ass out as she deserved.

I grabbed two beers from the little motel fridge that was tucked under the bathroom sink. I tossed one to Lilith before I started to get myself ready. I was mid-brushing my hair when I heard the door open. Looking in the mirror above the sink, I could see Melissa walk in.

She looked at Lilith like she knew she was caught. Trapped was more like it. Lilith grinned and held her beer can up in a "cheers" motion. I immediately forgot all my plans with Lilith. I no longer wanted to go out.

Stomping, I stormed over to Melissa and grabbed her by the throat, slamming her against the closed door. Lilith jumped up to get out of the way, making sure she didn't spill her beer.

"Where were you?" I snarled, my face inches from hers. I could smell the alcohol and cigarette smoke on her. I also smelled a hint of Drakkar Noir, a cologne I would not be caught dead wearing.

Melissa's cat eyes looked wildly at Lilith. Lilith just shrugged and sipped her beer. She was savoring the moment, enjoying the show. She hated Melissa.

"I just went for a couple of drinks with the girls after work," Melissa screeched. Always with her banshee screeching.

"And Greg?"

"Well…no…I mean…" she stammered, again looking at Lilith. Glaring was more like it. She knew Lilith ratted her out. Lilith just looked back at her amused, waiting to see how Melissa was going to lie her way out of this one.

"Look at me!" I screamed at her. I pulled her away from the door and threw her on the bed.

"No! He just tagged along. It was nothing!"

Lilith put her beer down on the dresser, among other empties and ashtrays.

"I'm out. I got to go. You coming with me, Heck?" she asked so casually as if my girlfriend and I were not in the middle of a fight.

I shook my head. I had to deal with Melissa.

"Okay. Suit yourself. Beep me if you want me to swing around," she said, letting herself out. "Otherwise, call me in the morning."

Melissa waited until the door shut behind Lilith, then focused her glare on me. She sat up, brushing her hair out of her face with her fingers.

"You fuckin' Greg?" I asked with a growl.

"No! That Lilith is a bitch! She's always telling you shit!"

I wanted to grab Melissa by her long hair and yank her head back. I refrained though, clenching my fists as rage surged through me. Instead, I lunged in front of her, my face only inches from hers, my jaw set on edge.

"You don't get to talk about her like that! She tells me the truth! She reminds me I'm living with a no-good slut!"

"Lies!" she screamed, her arms flailing at me, her nails trying to scratch at my face. I smacked her hands away.

"Did you fuck him?"

She didn't answer. I gave her a tap on her cheek.

"Did…you…fuck…him?"

Her crying turned to a laugh. She looked up at me, her dark eye make-up running down her cheeks as she peeked out from her messy hair.

"Did you fuck Lilith?" she asked. "I walked into our home and found you with another girl. Did you fuck her? See how that works, Heck?"

"You are crazy!"

"I'm crazy? Yeah, I am crazy because I put up with this weird *friendship* my boyfriend has with a crazy-ass lying bitch!" She used air quotes when she said friendship.

"Yeah? I'm not the one sticking my dick in Lilith," I told her. "But I am willing to bet Greg is sticking his in you!"

I gave her another light smack for good measure. Nothing hard.

It was just to make a point and have the last say. I left the room and wasn't surprised to see Lilith still out there in the motel parking lot in her van smoking a cigarette.

"I knew that wouldn't last," she laughed, opening the passenger door for me.

"She's such a lying cunt," I mumbled.

"She doesn't deserve you," she said, her grin slowly falling. "You deserve better. You always did. She can't handle you."

"Don't start this shit," I groaned. I knew where Lilith was heading. It was an old fight that surfaced every few months.

"Right," she agreed, starting up the van. She glanced over at me, her grin gone. She smiled gently. I hated it when she smiled at me like that, but I loved it too. No matter what, that smile told me how much she loved me. No one else ever smiled like that at me.

A car horn blared, and I was suddenly back in the traffic lane. The pace of the cars around me had picked up. I looked in my rearview mirror to see Destiny driving the car behind me. She looked at me amusingly and waggled her fingers with a tease.

I drove with the flow of traffic and continued my way to Melissa's mother's house. Eventually, Destiny disappeared from my view.

Melissa and I lasted another couple of months before calling it quits for good. It was with Lilith's help that our relationship ended. Lilith had spotted Melissa with that dumbass manager of hers in a car, going at it behind the video store. She raced to get me and bring me back so I could witness it myself.

Disgusted, Lilith and I went back to the motel. I packed my shit up and Lilith went to town taking a knife to all of Melissa's belongings: her clothes, her shoes, her bras and panties, even her purses. I dumped all of Melissa's make up in the tub and ran the water. Melissa's compact discs were scratched up or snapped in half. We left the room a complete disaster after I scrawled on the wall with lipstick "You're Greg's Now!"

Melissa never even tried to reach out to me after that. All the fighting and yelling and screeching came to a halt. It was over. And Lilith and I were together more than ever.

I pulled up in front of Melissa's house, surprised to see she was outside and about to get into her car. I gave her a little friendly honk and waved to get her attention. I saw how she stiffened up when she recognized me, her car keys clutched tightly in her hands.

"The fuck you want?" she greeted me as I exited my car to approach her. Yeah, this was not going to go well.

"Hey. Hi," I smiled, trying my best to turn on whatever it was that attracted her to me in the first place.

"I don't have time for your bullshit, Heck," she said. "I'm running late already."

"I just need to talk to you. Five minutes. I promise."

"We have nothing to say. You destroyed my shit! You and Lilith were two psychos that almost ruined me," she yelled.

"Oh, come on," I begged. "You weren't exactly the stellar example of a faithful girlfriend."

"Heck, I never cheated on you until the very end," she sighed. "I was so sick of you accusing me of cheating, of Lilith's little whispers in your ear constantly. You always believed her over me."

"Well, yeah," I shrugged. "She was my best friend."

"Well, yeah," Melissa mocked. "Your best friend is a liar. She started shit up with us all the fuckin' time, Heck! And what's even crazier? You knew it. You allowed it. You enjoyed it in some sick and twisted way. You both did."

She wasn't wrong. Lilith and I fed off of each other's drama like another addiction to our list of addictions. Lilith wouldn't lie to me though. Not then, anyway. I believed that.

"Look," I sighed. "Forget the past. We were both shitty to each other. But we are here now. This is my last moment with you and I want to make it a good one."

"What the hell are you babbling about, Heck?"

"I am trying my best to get my life together," I lied, starting the whole spiel. I was getting tired of it. Death couldn't come soon enough at this point. "I need to make amends. I've been going around, trying to talk to people I've done wrong and hurt. You being one of them."

"You were disgusting to me, Heck. I don't think you just get to say, 'I'm sorry' and everything is all hunky-dory. You hit me, Heck. You hurt me physically and mentally."

"You hit me too. You fought like a drowning cat! I think I still have scars from your nails scratching at me," I joked, making little cat claw hands and hissing noises.

She gave me a small smile. It was working. I was cracking her.

"I guess I did get some good jabs in here and there," she said. "But still…"

"Look. You are like…you are the road to a better future for me. To keep myself from resorting to such awful abuse again, I need your forgiveness. I need closure."

I would have to thank Julia for putting the whole "closure" bullshit idea in my head.

Melissa sighed. She searched my face, trying to see if there were any signs of lies. I kept my face as straight as I could and stared back at her. Her teal eyes were so intense.

"I don't know, Heck. I guess," she finally said. "Just leave me alone after this. Promise me that."

I broke out with a big smile. I was winning. Heaven was just around the corner. I opened my arms to hug her, but she backed away with her hand out and shook her head. I didn't blame her. I began to walk back to the car when she called out to me.

"You and Lilith ever get together?"

I stopped and turned around, shaking my head.

"It was never like that," I said. "You know that."

"You gonna make amends with her?"

"Actually, she's next on my list," I admitted. I had to chuckle to myself because there really was a list.

"You should be with her. You two deserve each other."

"Too late for that. But thanks for the advice," I said sarcastically before getting in the car and driving off.

With my eyes on the road, I pulled out the card Destiny had handed me at the hospital. Only one name. Lilith Patton.

She was going to be the easiest one. Of all the girls on the list, I never once worried about Lilith. Despite our falling out, she was always my best friend. No matter what, she was always there for me. There was no way she would not forgive me. She loved me.

VI.

Just over one full day left and only one name left. Lilith Patton. My ex-best friend. The one girl who truly saw me. And saw through me. The one girl who was not afraid of me, my temper, or my rage. The one girl who was able to give it to me just as badly as I gave it to her. We were two rotten peas in a pod, cast from the same mold of insanity.

I headed towards Lilith's house, wondering where I was going to see the sarcastic Destiny today. How would she present herself? Would she be a cashier in a random deli or maybe even a cop to pull me over? It did not matter because Lilith would wipe that evil grin right off that Devil Bitch's face. Lilith was my ticket to glorious eternity. Lilith would always love me. She would always take me back. She would always forgive me because Lilith saw herself in me.

I started to shift into the haze of memory. I was surprised it was happening so soon. Maybe Destiny knew the game was almost over. The thirty-odd hours to find Lilith were not needed. I would get that forgiveness and then I could spend my final night partying it up before my eventual demise.

The fog cleared and I was pumping gas at a gas station. It was my job before I started towing cars. It was also where my friendship with Lilith began.

Lilith and I had known each other practically all our lives. We went to school together, starting back in kindergarten. But we were never friends. Just classmates.

On the day our friendship began, she was a high school graduate while I was a high school dropout. I pumped gas to make some bucks, but Lilith? She had a unique business, and somewhat illegal.

Lilith was smart, despite being crazy. She had a great use of English vocabulary and understood proper writing grammar more than the average high school teacher in our neighborhood. Lilith took her smarts and used them to write school papers for other students, for a price. She made pretty decent money doing it, too.

I could see her arguing with some kid, a small stack of typed papers in his hands. He was laughing and she looked pissed. I recognized Lilith from our school days before I dropped out. She looked the same. Nondescript straight brown hair framed her plain face. Dressed in jeans and a rock concert T-shirt. Motorcycle boots on her feet.

I was amused when Lilith started screaming and got up in the kid's face. She reached to grab the papers back from him, but he just held them high. He was pretty tall compared to her. I was shocked when she balled up a fist and took a swing at him.

"Holy shit!" I laughed. The kid ducked and gave her a shove. Not a hard one that would have sent her on her ass, but enough to make her stumble back and put distance between the two of them.

I rushed over to them. I don't know what compelled me to get involved. Fights were not uncommon in Garden Hollows, but something made me want to help her. Maybe it was because, once upon a time, we were classmates. Maybe it was because I was bored.

"Hey!" I yelled, approaching them. "What's going on here?"

Lilith looked over her shoulder at me and frowned with confusion.

She recognized me, though. It wasn't that long ago we sat in the same math class.

"I did a paper for him and now he won't pay up," she grumbled.

"I told you." The kid whined with a roll of his eyes. "I'll pay you when I get my grades."

"And I told you." She shot back, "I get paid when I give you the paper!"

"Nuh-uh," he laughed. "How do I know I'm gonna pass? I need to pass this semester. I need a perfect score."

"And that's what you are paying for. I guarantee you a perfect score!"

"Dick," I said, "Just pay her. Don't be an asshole."

"Who the fuck are you?" he asked, glancing at me.

"Her friend. Just pay her. Everyone knows her word is good. Everyone knows her papers are worth it."

"Fuck this," I heard Lilith say. I looked over and saw her reach into her back pocket and pull out a switchblade. She clicked the button and the long, slim, lethal but beautiful blade popped out.

"Give me back my fucking paper," she growled. Her violet eyes sparkled with both anger and delight. I realized she was enjoying the drama. She loved that she had an excuse to pull her blade out.

"Wait, hold on…alright," the kid stammered. "I'll pay."

He wasn't afraid of the knife. It was Lilith that frightened him. He saw it too in her eyes. This little woman was downright scary. She was grinning despite her anger.

"No," she said. "You don't deserve it. I don't work hard for assholes like you."

"Oh, come on!"

I took the opportunity to grab the papers from him. Lilith laughed and made a little threatening stabbing motion with the blade.

"You should go," I said, my voice deepened to intimidate the kid. "Before we both beat the shit out of you."

He groaned and grumbled, but he walked away. I turned to Lilith, smiling like we just won a great battle and not some dumb neighborhood corner conflict. I glanced down at the paper and saw the title. "Hamlet: A Tale of an Oedipus Complex." I had no idea what that was about, nor did I care. It was way over my head.

"Thanks, Heck," she said, putting her blade back in the back pocket of her jeans. From her other pocket, she pulled out a pack of smokes. Being the nice guy I am, I offered to light it, then lit up one of my own. I handed her the paper back.

"Sorry you lost out on money with that dick," I said.

"Nah," she shook her head. "It's all good. I can sell it to someone else. Just type up a new cover page with their name."

"That's cool. My brother is still in school. Maybe I can have him ask around for you," I offered.

"Yeah, that would be great. Thanks."

We stood there, smoking our cigarettes and making small talk. It all ended when my boss popped his head out of the gas station to wave me back to work. Lilith and I exchanged beeper numbers and walked our separate ways.

The fog cleared. I was still driving toward Lilith's house. It was only a couple of blocks away.

That one afternoon at the gas station set off the friendship. She began making her "drops," as she called them, on that corner a regular thing. It was never spoken, but we both knew it was so I could keep an eye on things in case an exchange went south again. More often than not, kids thought they could walk away without paying her or offering her a lower price than what was agreed upon. Most of the time Lilith was able to handle it herself.

We would hang out more and more in between me pumping gas for random cars. Sometimes, we would grab a bite to eat together on my breaks. Then she offered to do a paper for Freddie, free of charge. The next thing I knew, we were all hanging out after work and school hours. Her house. My house. The park. Driving in cars. Our friends intermingled. We became one big group. This continued for a couple of years. Most of it was drama and fighting, but we were always friends in the end. Until the end.

I pulled up at Lilith's house. It had been so long since I had been there. It became a second home to me until we had our big fight.

It was a big, old, run-down farmhouse on a big lot. The farm was long gone for at least fifty years or more. Now, the house was surrounded by overgrowth and parked cars here and there. The front porch had an old couch for hanging out. The shutters were crooked around the windows.

It looked like a trash house that needed a lot of work and clean up, but the truth was, once inside, it was home. It was more of a home than the one I grew up in.

I had not even gotten out of the car yet when the fog started to come back. I tried to shake my head and clear my mind to fight it. It was weird. None of the other names had a second memory. Why was I falling down that rabbit hole again? The haze was not letting up.

It cleared and it was a chilly Christmas Eve night. Lilith's house was decorated outside with some colored lights wrapped around the porch railings. There was a tree in the living room. Christmas music blared from the stereo. It was some old-time crooner like Bing Crosby. It was comforting.

Lilith and I had been friends for months by now. Her mom had invited me to their traditional Christmas Eve party. It was not like I had seen in the movies. There was no roaring fire in the fireplace or eggnog in a bowl. No Christmas ham with all the fixings. But it was still something.

The house was crowded with people having a good time. That was Lilith's house. Her house was where people always seemed to gather and hang out and have a good time. It was not a fancy home, but it was a clean and comfortable home.

Lilith's mom was everything my mother was not. Sure, she had her issues with alcohol, and she loved her weed, but she was a nice drunk. She was a functional drunk.

Suzy was a product of the late 1960's and never let go of her hippie views and lifestyle. Lilith's house was an eclectic one with odd mismatch furniture collected over the years and items displayed as art, but was not really art. There were always lots of candles or incense burning. Tapestries draped the walls. And people were always in and out. Especially men. Suzy was the type of woman who could not go without a relationship. Lilith had many "step" fathers in her life.

Lilith had two sisters and a brother, all of them from different fathers. Not one of them knew their father either. Lilith and her siblings all pretty much got along but were not best friends like some siblings were. They did not hang out with us like her cousin, Heather, or my brother, Freddie. They were not part of our circle.

"Got you something," Lilith smiled, reaching under the tree and grabbing a wrapped box.

"Oh, come one," I said, actually blushing. I could not remember the last time someone bought me a Christmas present. "I don't exchange gifts."

"That's okay," she said, grabbing my hand. She pulled me up the stairs, past some people sharing a joint. We headed to her room, and she shut the door behind her.

Her room was her own, the house large enough so nobody had to share. It was cluttered, like most bedrooms I had been in, including my own. Unlike my room though, she had a desk with a word processor for her paper writing. There were piles of paper and spiral-bound notebooks next to it. If you looked around her room, you could see books piled everywhere. Some were from the library to help with her next paper. Most were her own. Her walls were adorned with posters of rock bands, and an Aerosmith banner covered her window, acting as a curtain. Among her ashtrays and empty cigarette packs were odd items: a skull from some animal, twisted bundles of sage, different colored crystals, and strange candles. Nothing out of the norm for someone who was trying to be edgy.

It was not out of the ordinary for Lilith and me to escape to her room. Her house was always filled with people of all ages hanging out. Her room was her place to be alone. It was quickly becoming my place to be alone too. She even had a flip chair and extra blankets and pillows for me to crash on from time to time.

I sat on her bed, and she handed me my gift. It was not anything big. Just a Black Sabbath t-shirt she most likely found at a flea market and a CD of one of their albums. But it was still cool. More importantly, it felt nice to get a Christmas gift.

"Oh, wow!" I exclaimed, holding the shirt up to my chest. "This is awesome! Thank you!"

I wrapped my arms around her and hugged her. We sat there for a moment. She pulled away a little and looked up at me. Her violet eyes were searching for something. I could feel the tension begin to get thick between us.

"Why aren't we together?" she suddenly asked.

I was not expecting that. We had become fast friends. We never once came close to being physical other than casual friendly arms slung around each other.

I pulled back from her, pushing her away from me. She was confusing me. Her eyes immediately went dark showing she was suddenly pissed.

"Really, Lilith?" I asked. "Don't do this. We got a good thing. You are my friend. I don't want to ruin that."

"We are together every single day," she reminded me. "What are we doing wrong?"

"No. I mean…" I didn't know how to answer her. I did not know how to tell her that she scared me. No girl scared me as she did. She was always by my side and supportive and accepting. She had my back no matter what. She was the only person who was not afraid of my mother's antics when she came over to my house. She was the only girl that was not afraid of me when I went off on my psycho rages. She was the only person that encouraged me, even in my darkest moments. She enjoyed my dark moments. That was what scared me. I could not intimidate her, and she could not intimidate me. We were two toxic souls that would implode on one another like a cosmic collision if we became more than friends. Our friendship balanced on a very fine line between sanity and insanity.

I shrugged, folding the shirt and putting it back in the box.

"I can't lose you," I finally said, not sure if that was a lie or the truth. "I never had a friend like you. You are more than a friend to me. You are family. My only family, really. Please, let's not ruin this."

She nodded, getting up from the bed. Bending down, she placed a kiss on my cheek.

"I'll give you time," she said with a sudden grin.

"No, Lilith—"

I was cut off by my beeper vibrating. Lilith's went off only seconds after. It was Freddie. He had scored some good blow and was looking to share.

"I guess it's a White Christmas!" Lilith sang with a laugh, leaving her bedroom with a little skip.

The fog cleared, but the memory remained on the surface of my brain. I smiled to myself, looking at Lilith's beat-up house. I realized it was not run down. It was just wear and tear from years of being a home for anyone who needed it, including myself.

That Christmas ended up being fun. We spent the night doing lines in Lilith's room and hanging out with all sorts of people throughout the rest of the house. There might not have been a fireplace, but Lilith's brother and his friends started a huge bonfire in the yard. Folding chairs were brought out from the garage. Lilith's mom passed out blankets for us to get cozy under. All sorts of drinks and even a bowl that was endlessly packed with weed were passed around.

I crashed in my usual spot-on Lilith's floor and woke up Christmas afternoon to Suzy making pancakes. Lilith and her family exchanged presents and Lilith's mom even had a gift for me, which was sweet. It felt great to be included, to feel loved.

I gathered myself together. It was time to face Lilith. I wondered if maybe this was where I was meant to be when I died. Lilith's house would be a nice place to die. Maybe that was why I had two memories. To remind me of how good I had it.

I walked up the old wooden steps and rang the doorbell. I was looking forward to seeing Lilith again. Our last fight was a rough one. It was more than a fight. There were so many layers to it, but I knew Lilith. Even if I had to lie and tell her I loved her the way she always wanted me to love her, she would take me back.

The door opened and Lilith's mother stood before me. Her long, graying hippie hair was pulled back on the sides, held with beaded clips. She wore a long sweater and a long, prairie-girl skirt. Her feet were bare, even though it was cold. She looked tired. Exhausted. A frown was set on her face that seemed to have been there for a long time. This was not the vibrant, free-spirited woman I knew a year ago. She looked at me like she hated me.

"Mom?" I asked. I rarely called my own mother that, but after that Christmas, I began to call Suzy that. She was more of a mom to me than my own mother was. She was everyone's mother. So many neighborhood kids called her mom.

"You know better than to call me that," she muttered. I don't think I ever heard her speak with a tone of disdain before.

"Oh," I said, kind of saddened by that. "Okay, Suzy. Lilith

around?"

She looked at me, surprised and confused. She still had that hateful look though.

"You don't know?" she asked.

"Know what?"

"Lilith's gone."

This was news to me. No one told me Lilith left. Maybe finding her was going to be harder than I thought.

"Where did she go?"

"She left after you two…" she trailed off, looking into the distance. She suddenly shook her head. "You know what. You don't deserve to know. She wouldn't want you to know."

She slammed the door on me, leaving me alone on the front porch bewildered.

"What the fuck?!"

What was once my happy place was suddenly rejecting me. I was just a stranger on a strange porch. I pounded the door with my fists.

"Mom! Suzy! Come on!" I yelled. She never turned anyone away, but she was turning me away. "Fuck you! You crazy pot-head hippie!"

Yeah. That was not going to get me any points with Lilith, but I was pissed. She had no right to keep me from knowing where Lilith was. To keep me from Lilith.

I walked back to the car, kicking a rock in frustration. Getting in, I slammed the door violently. I needed to think. I needed to think about who would know where Lilith was. Her sisters. Her brother. Heather.

Morella was Lilith's oldest sister. She had moved out some time ago to the local trailer park with her boyfriend and their baby. She would know where Lilith was. She would tell me.

I headed over to the trailer park, my eyes peeled for a sighting of Destiny. So far, she had not made her appearance. The ride was uneventful. No Destiny. No foggy haze of fucked up memories.

I knew which trailer was Morella's. Lilith and I had visited once or twice when Morella first moved into it. It was a small one-bedroom trailer at the end of the lot. I remembered Morella bragging that the end of the lot was the best spot because they had no neighbors to the left of them. She was talking like she and her dumb boyfriend just scored a mansion on sprawling grounds.

The trailer was old and beat up. There was a picnic table right outside the door and toddler toys strewn about, mixed in with beer cans and bottles. A dream yard for a trailer trash child.

The door flew open before I could even step out of the car. Morella came out on the stoop. She was largely pregnant again. Her little girl peeked out from behind her legs.

"No," she yelled. "Nope! My mother already called me. I know why you are here, and the answer is no. We ain't telling you shit, Heck!"

"What the fuck?" I asked myself for what was probably the millionth time that week.

She was not budging. And I did not need her calling the cops on me. I couldn't afford to spend time down at the station. Not to mention I may or may not have a warrant for my arrest since I left the hospital under suspicious circumstances. I was not even sure about that and where I stood with the law. Shit, I probably had other warrants that I had forgotten about.

Sighing, I lit a cigarette. I had to think. Lilith's other sister was still out there somewhere. I remembered she was a waitress at a local greasy spoon coffee shop. I guess that was my next stop. Hopefully, she was still working there, and it was her shift. Her being at home, holed up with her mom would be no help for me. I bet the coffee shop would be where Destiny would present herself to me. I could picture her wearing one of the cheesy waitress uniforms while she taunted me.

The coffee shop was one whose clientele was made up of blue-collar men and high school students. It was usually the busiest at breakfast and the slowest at dinner. It was small, and the décor was the same avocado green and brown since the early 1970s.

I walked in to see it was not that busy and Lilith's sister, Verona, was hanging by the counter chit-chatting with some guy who was wearing a dark blue jumper with a plumber's logo embroidered on the back. This was not the type of place where you waited to be seated, so I continued to walk in and went straight up to Verona.

Of all of Lilith's siblings, Verona looked the most like her with her straight brown hair. Unlike Lilith though, Verona took the time every day to put her hair in the latest styles and do a full face of make-up. Lilith was always more into the natural look, very little, if any, make-up, and long hair was usually free from scrunchies, hair clips, and sticky products.

"Hey, Verona," I greeted, tapping her on the shoulder. She turned around, a smile already on her face. It fell quickly when she saw me. "Can I talk to you for a sec?"

"I have nothing to say to you," she shook her head, starting to walk away. I reached out to grab her, but the plumber she was talking to glared at me. I was not taking the chance of getting him involved. He looked huge, sitting there on the counter stool.

"Look," I begged, following her as she walked around and ripped the paper from her order pad, dropping them on people's tables. She ignored me, staying focused on her job, smiling at the customers and telling them "Thank you" and "Have a nice day."

Then, she spun around to face me.

"You need to leave. We don't want anything to do with you. You need to go," she insisted, her hands on her hips.

"I just want to know where Lilith is. Your mother says she moved," I told her. "Even just a phone number would be fine."

Would a phone number suffice in this game of Heaven or Hell?

Would a phone call to Lilith be enough or would I have to see her face-to-face for forgiveness to count? I did not even know what Destiny's rules were anymore. I was desperate to get this last name off of my list so I could go get drunk and high and die in peace.

"I don't have to tell you shit," she said.

"Then, I will just sit here and stay until you do," I threatened, sliding into a booth. "I'm not leaving. I'll stay and be a good little customer, but I ain't leaving until you tell me where to find Lilith. Shit, call her right now and tell her to meet me here. I need to talk to her. I'm not going to do anything to her or whatever bullshit is going through your head."

Verona sighed and pointed to the clock above the counter. It was sandwiched between a breakfast menu and a lunch menu. The prices had been changed over the years using masking tape and a permanent black marker.

"It's noon," she said. She untied her green apron. "You can stay all day for all I care. I'm done. My shift is over. Don't you dare fuckin' follow me, Heck, because I will have my boss call the police."

I dropped my head in my hands in defeat. I could not win. What did I expect? I never could win when it came to Lilith. It should not surprise me that she was playing hide and seek with me. She most likely got word of me going around from Heather, and her whole family was in on this sick little game of hers. Lilith loved to play her twisted games with people. We were always her amusement.

Verona had walked away and in her place was another girl wearing the same shit brown uniform. She had her pad and pen ready to take my order. My stomach growled and I remembered I had not eaten since before my drive to Julia's. I was starving and I had time. I still had Lilith's little brother to find. If he was a good kid, he was still in school. I could catch him outside the high school when it let out. He was a skinny little shit, easy to intimidate. He would tell me what I needed to know.

I ordered their largest breakfast platter and a coffee. I was not just starving, I was ravenous. I wondered if it was because I had not eaten or if it was because I was also drug and alcohol-free for more than 24 hours. Or maybe it was something to do with death coming for me in 36 hours. Maybe my body was going into some sort of weird survival mode. Whatever it was, eggs, pancakes, potatoes, and three different types of breakfast meats sounded pretty fuckin' delicious to me.

My coffee came immediately. I added six little packets of sugar and stirred it. The whirlpool of black coffee began to mesmerize me. Round and round it went as I spiraled deeper and deeper into it. It was happening again. For the third time that day, a memory was sweeping me away.

I was at a house party. It was loud, dark, and smoky like all parties. The rooms were packed, people on top of each other and in each other's faces. The air was thick with smoke from the cigarettes and the four-foot bong in the corner that was being enjoyed by a small group of people. It smelled not only of weed but wisps of hair products and spilled alcohol. Guns and Roses played at top volume while people talked and laughed loudly to be heard. There was no reason for celebrating. It was not someone's birthday or a holiday. Just another Saturday night at some parentless house.

I was with Melissa. It was early in our relationship, and we had not yet made the regretful decision to move into the dumpy roadside motel. I held her hand and navigated through the throngs of people. I could see my friends and Freddie sitting at the dining room table playing cards, ashtrays, and bottles and cans everywhere on the table. Lilith was off to the side talking to some guy I'd never seen before. She saw me with Melissa and smiled. I nodded to her.

I grabbed a seat, taking Melissa into my lap. I could feel Lilith's eyes on us as she continued to talk to the strange guy. I leaned over to Mitch and asked him who the guy was.

"Dunno. He showed up a little bit before you did. Why?" Mitch asked without looking up from dealing the deck and his cigarette dangling from his lips.

"Just wondering," I muttered. I was not sure why I wanted to know either.

"I know him," Melissa said. "He's a dealer. But he only deals when he needs money. Not like full-time or anything. And he only sells trips. Nothing else."

"What's his name?"

"Jimmy, I think," she said.

I looked back over at Lilith. She was no longer looking at Melissa and me. She was completely focused on this Jimmy guy. I recognized that light, flirty half-smile on her face. The smile that screamed, "I'm not really interested in a single word you are saying, but I am *interested*."

He was her type, that's for sure. Tall and thin. Long hair. Jeans and t-shirt kind of guy. Not much different from me, except for the tall part. Hair was lighter too. But still, just your all-American rock and roll white trash guy. Like me.

I should have been happy for Lilith. She had been acting odd since Melissa and I started dating. I knew she wished we were more than friends, but she had to know by now that that was all we would ever be. I should have been happy that Lilith was talking to someone and having a good time. That there was a light flirtation going on between the two of them.

But I wasn't. I don't know why, but it was irritating me. It was making me jumpy under my skin. And the thought of her getting serious with this Jimmy or any other guy meant the end of our friendship. There was no way a boyfriend would put up with us being friends. Not with the way we fight and push each other's buttons. Not with the way we had each other's backs. Our friendship was a unique one. I would lose her.

I tried to concentrate on the card game, on the music, on the jokes being thrown about the table, and most importantly on my girlfriend that sat in my lap. I nuzzled her neck, making her giggle, and rubbed her side, her thighs, and her back. Anything to get me in the mood to maybe take Melissa to an empty room somewhere. It was not working, though. I could not get my mind straight.

I felt my beeper go off and maneuvered around Melissa to get it out of my pocket. 666. That was Lilith's and my code. I looked up to see she was gone. How long had she been gone? 666 usually meant we scored our drug of choice: blow. I was intrigued. Maybe she was not just flirting with this Jimmy. Melissa did say he was a dealer. Maybe he had blow and Lilith got some off of him. Whatever it was, I was going to find out. I could use the fix.

"Be right back," I said, practically lifting Melissa off my lap.

"Where you going?"

"Bathroom," I lied. I did not need her with me. This was Lilith's and my thing first. Depending on how much Lilith was able to get, we would decide if we wanted to share it. It always went this way. It was sort of an unspoken deal Lilith and I had together.

I walked around, searching the living room, kitchen, and television room for Lilith. I went into the basement where even more people were crowded in. It was a total disaster down there, the bar completely ransacked. Someone was going to get their ass kicked when their parents came home.

I pulled someone aside and asked them if they saw Lilith. They shook their heads. Walking back up the stairs, I asked a few more people. Someone finally answered me.

"Saw her go up," a girl said, jerking her thumb to motion up the stairs.

I thanked her and headed up. Upstairs was empty and quieter. I opened doors carefully to peek in. There was the master bedroom that belonged to the homeowners. I assumed the second bedroom belonged to the kid who threw the party. One door led to a laundry closet. All were void of Lilith. I frowned, wondering where she was. There was only one door left.

I opened it quietly, just to peek in, expecting it to be empty like the other rooms. Blood immediately rushed to my face and my eyes went wide and my mouth opened when I saw Lilith. She was bent over, holding onto an office chair. She had not a stitch of clothing on, her breasts swaying as Jimmy slammed into her from behind. He pumped violently, one hand on her hip and the other entwined in her long brown hair, holding her in place.

She looked up and straight at me, a look of pure pleasure on her face. She locked her eyes with me, causing me to become still. I could not move. I could barely breathe as the air became thick and weighed heavily on my chest. She smiled and bit her bottom lip at the same time, moaning with mounting ecstasy. I realized I was completely aroused. I wanted to burst in and knock Jimmy aside and take his place to finish her.

She never looked away from me watching from the little open slit of the doorway. She kept her eyes on me as she continued to be rocked by Jimmy. Her face said it all. She was enjoying all of it with every fiber of her being. And me being there, watching like a creeper, made it even better for her.

I don't think I had ever been so engorged before. I felt like I was going to burst right then and there in my jeans as she became more and more vocal. One last explosive grunt and she came. He finished only seconds after her.

She stood there, panting and her legs a little shaky. Lilith still watched me. She did not even turn around to say a word to Jimmy as he removed himself from her and walked away. He went into another room that I assumed was a bathroom.

Smiling like a satisfied cat, Lilith finally let go of the chair and walked over to me. I could not speak. I was still so fuckin' hard.

She opened the door wider and stood just inches away from me, completely nude. I could smell Jimmy on her.

She looked up at me, her grin still there, her breath still trying to steady itself. She reached out and traced my crotch through my jeans with her fingertips. She laughed.

"I thought so," she said before turning away and shutting the door on me.

The memory cleared and I realized I was sitting in the coffee shop, completely excited. I shifted in my seat uncomfortably and could feel the heat on my face. Someone slid into the seat across from me. Destiny. Of course, it was Destiny.

"Got a little hard-on going there, don't you?" she grinned. "That was a good memory, huh?"

"Goddamn you," I muttered, my voice a little squeaky. The waitress came with my plates of food and then asked Destiny if she would like anything.

"Blueberry pancakes and strawberry syrup please," Destiny said.

"That's Lilith's favorite," I told her.

"I know."

"Is there anything you don't know? Maybe you could tell me where Lilith is and just make this a little bit easier for me?"

"Oh," she giggled. "Where's the fun in that?"

I dunked my toast in the eggs, slopping up the gooey yellow yolk.

"Maybe you don't know everything," I said, biting the toast. I could feel the yolk dribble down my chin. "Because if you knew Lilith as well as you think you do, you would know that Lilith loves me. Like...*loves me loves me.* This is all just game to her right now, but in the end, when I find her, and I will find her, she will forgive me and all will be right with us for my final earthly hours."

"True," she nodded. "She does love you. Ever think she loves you too much?"

"Is there such a thing?"

"I don't know. You tell me."

She was being cryptic again. Another bitch that loved to play games. Maybe if I ignored her, she would just zap away.

"Tell me," she began as her plate of pancakes was placed in front of her, "Why did you watch? Why didn't you walk away?"

"I dunno," I shrugged with a mouth full of potatoes. "Why didn't she stop? Why didn't she yell out and tell me to shut the fuckin' door? She watched me watch her."

My head was spinning with this conversation.

"Hmmm…" she trailed off, "So, you both play games. That's a healthy friendship."

"Get out of my fuckin' head!" I yelled. People stopped talking and stared at us. She just laughed and happily cut into her blueberry pancakes. I was beginning to lose my appetite.

"Please," I begged, lowering my voice and leaning in. "I just want to eat in peace. This might very well be my last meal."

Her grin fell. Her eyes softened. Was this sympathy she was suddenly looking at me with? She nodded sadly and continued to eat her pancakes.

"What's it like?" I asked. "The other side? Heaven and Hell?"

"Depends on you and how you lived your life here," she said.

"Come on," I groaned. "No stupid puzzling answers."

"No, really. I'm being straight with you, Heck. Heaven is whatever makes you happy here on Earth. Hell is whatever made you miserable. Not much of a difference if you ask me."

"Great. Not much made me happy and everything makes me miserable," I sighed.

"You don't seem too upset about dying," she said.

"Been dying my whole damn life," I shrugged. "It was coming for me sooner or later."

"You're not afraid?"

"Just of hell. Afraid if there's any pain," I admitted.

"If it makes you feel any better, physical pain is too easy. It eventually numbs you. Be more afraid of the madness. Hell gets creative," she spoke with a sharp whisper. Her eyes were looking at me with such intensity that she was giving me the creeps.

I wiped my mouth with a cheap paper napkin. There was still about half of a plate of food left but as starving as I was, I lost my appetite. I stood up, tossing some crumbled bills that I had found in my pocket onto the table.

"Heck, I'm going to leave you alone," she said, pushing her plate away. "You don't have much time and you still have a ton to figure out. Not just with finding Lilith and all that. But you need to figure yourself out."

"Nothing to figure out. I'm a dick. Always was and always will be, at least for the next…" I glanced up at the clock. "Thirty-five and a half hours anyway. But she will forgive me."

"If you say so." Her singsong teasing and taunting voice were back. I swear, she was the devil.

I walked out of the coffee shop into the grey and chilly day. I flipped my collar up on my leather jacket. I remembered this was the same leather jacket Lilith had bought for me on my 21st birthday, right before our big fallout. Our friendship did not last as long as it seemed. It felt like years, and it was, but not the long years. Not the decades. Just three measly years which was nothing in the grand scheme of time.

I hit up a payphone to beep one of my many dealers. I needed to keep my energy up. I arranged for him to meet me at the park across from the high school. I figured I would keep myself busy while I waited for school to let out and then I could try and track down Lilith's little brother, Bo.

The deal was made. Just a small amount, twisted into a bundle of plastic wrap. I carefully scooped up a tiny, little pile with my key. One big sniff up the right nostril. I repeated the process with the left one.

I breathed in deeply and relished the odd but lovely feeling of the drip from the back of my nose down my throat. It was cold and slightly numbing. The best feeling ever. Maybe that would be my Heaven. Nothing but blow everywhere. And sex. Lots of sex with hot girls that looked as if they were straight from the latest music video. My Heaven would have music too. Good, feel-it-in-your-blood rock music. None of that bubble-gum, pop crap. My Heaven would be everything that America was made of: Sex, Drugs, and Rock and Roll. That's all I needed.

I turned on the radio, chewing on the inside cheek of my mouth. Lilith always said that was my tell-tale sign that I was wired. She would always tease me about it, wondering why I did not have a hole in my face yet. I nodded my head to the beat of the song. It was a classic by Metallica, one of my favorite bands.

The fog came again. This time it was quick and sucked me right in. My chest pounded as I slammed into the memory. I had the sensation of falling and suddenly jerking like I was in a dream.

Lilith and I were in my living room. It was one of the few times my mother was not sprawled on the couch hogging the television. We were drinking, eating some Chinese food take-out that Lilith had picked up, and watching a video she rented. It was some movie with Johnny Depp and scissors. I wasn't paying attention. Lilith was much more into it.

I heard a car pull up and turn off. A car door slammed shut. I groaned. She was home. My mother stumbled in, surprisingly decently dressed. That only meant one thing. She was missing my father and decided to visit him at the state penitentiary.

"Hey, Annie," Lilith called out. She was always kind and polite to my mother. "Got some Chinese. Want some?"

My mother groaned and plopped herself down in the armchair, barely moving the blankets and pillows Lilith had piled there so we could sit on her couch.

"I can't eat," she started. "Your goddamn father wouldn't see me today. I drove all the way up there! Two fuckin' hours up there and two fuckin' hours back and that damn bastard refused my visit!"

"Ugh," Lilith said, taking the remote and pausing the movie. I rolled my eyes. I would much rather figure out why a man had scissors for hands than listen to my mother go on and on about my father. "I'm sorry to hear that. That sucks."

"What's that you are drinking?" my mother asked, pointing to Lilith's bottle. Leave it up to her to zoom right in on the booze.

"Zima."

"What's that? A soda?"

"No, Mom," I said with annoyance. "It's not a soda. It's the latest drink."

"You want to try one?" Lilith asked her.

"Why are you encouraging this shit?" I groaned.

"Oh, shut up, Hecky," my mother said, holding her hand out for Lilith to pass her a bottle. She took a sip and frowned. "What is this shit? Taste like stale lemon-lime soda."

Lilith laughed and reached over to the side table where a round-shaped bottle of raspberry-flavored liquor sat. She leaned over to my mother and carefully poured a little into the Zima bottle, turning the clear liquid into a pinkish-purple color.

"Now try it," she said.

My mother's eyes lit, and she gulped down half the bottle.

"That is yummy!" she laughed. "What are you two kids doing at home? Why ain't you out and about, painting the town red? You should take Lilith out somewhere nice. Treat her to someplace special."

"Not now, Annie," I warned.

"You two still ain't fuckin'? Lord, what are you waiting for?"

"Annie cut the shit!" I screamed. Lilith put her hand on my arm, her signal to tell me to calm down.

"Not like that, Ann, you know that," Lilith said softly. I detected a hint of sadness in her voice. "Besides, Heck just moved back home from Melissa."

"Bitch," Mom muttered. "Never liked her."

"Me either," Lilith smiled, raising her bottle. My mother laughed and clinked it.

"I don't get it though. You two are so much alike, except you are nicer, Lilith."

"She only pretends to be nice," I quipped.

"Well, at least she's nice to me," my mother claimed.

"She's faking it."

Lilith hit me on the arm this time to tell me to shut up.

"See!" my mother pointed. "She knows how to handle you. Keeps you in your place. You two should get married."

"What the fuck?" I cried out as Lilith burst out laughing. "Jesus Christ, Mom! We are just friends!"

"I'll pay you. I'm not kidding. I can pay you if you marry him. Take him off my hands," she continued as Lilith just kept laughing.

"Pay her?! With what money?"

"I got money," she shot at me.

"Really? This is news to me. Where's the money, Annie? Because you barely paid the electric bill this month!"

"I can get money!"

"Where? Maybe if you cash in all the cans and bottles that are thrown all over the place."

"Hey! Whoa!" Lilith said, still smiling. "Come on. I'm here to have a good time. No need to start with each other. Annie, you look out. Want another drink?"

"I need something harder," she grumbled getting up.

"How about this?" Lilith said, pulling a dime bag from her pocket. My mother smiled.

"I always liked her," she said. "I'm making some Jack and Cokes to go with it. You want one, son?"

I calmed down. It was not my idea of a good time, hanging out with Lilith and my mother. Things would eventually turn nasty. It always did when it came to my mother. But I nodded, accepting the drink offer. I had no idea why I was going along with this. This should have been my cue to tell Lilith we needed to either move it to my room or take the party back to her house. However, I stayed. Maybe I needed to embrace these moments because they were so far and few.

Lilith cleared a spot on the coffee table to roll the joint. I could hear ice clinking in glasses in the kitchen and prayed my mother reached for some clean glasses from the cabinet and not one of the many dirty ones that have been sitting for God knows how long on the kitchen counter.

"Now it's a party!" she sang, coming back with three tall glasses filled with ice and brown liquid. She set them down to run back and grab the bottle of generic cola and Jack, so we didn't have to get up to make refills. God forbid we were inconvenienced by getting up and walking the whole five feet to the kitchen to make more drinks.

The room filled with the sweet smoky air and the drinks were refilled before we finished them. We chased some of them with just pure shots of Jack. We had the occasional Zima mixed with raspberry liquor. Lilith helped herself to my mother's old collection of albums and put Creedence Clearwater Revival on the turntable. Things were getting weird as Lilith and my mom were up dancing and laughing, having a good time.

It was not just weird. It was actually nice, which made it weird. It was nice not having my mother screaming and cursing at me, calling me names. It was nice that Lilith was able to get along with her, which seemed almost impossible for most people. As drunk and stoned as we were, it felt normal. My mother was telling old stories and they were interesting and sometimes funny. I had forgotten that my mother was someone who, at one time long ago, had a sense of humor. I remember there was a time, when I was very little, that my mother made people laugh in her loud and boisterous way. This was a very brief time before my father was sent off, leaving her to fend for herself and two young boys. This was a time, long forgotten, before she just gave up.

We were deep into the night, the dime bag all smoked and the Jack bottle empty and replaced with some cheap vodka. We were drinking slower, and conversation was becoming less and less frequent.

I moved to the chair so my mother could take her rightful spot on the couch. The music was turned off and the movie was turned back on. Lilith stood next to me, quiet and looking down at me, her violet eyes so intense. I could feel her searching for something within me.

I was drunk. I was high. I was caught up in the night. I reached out and took her hand, pulling her down into my lap. There was another chair, but it was covered in litter, as it always was. I felt bad Lilith had no place to sit.

We sat like that for a moment, staring straight at the television. I could feel the thickness in the air between Lilith and me. I shifted my weight a little under her, pulling her even closer. She rested her head on my chest.

It still felt nice. Normal. And yet weird. I did not want this.

She tilted her head up to me. I looked away from Johnny Depp with his crazy hair and looked down at her. I could see the booze and weed in her eyes. I could also see that she felt the thickness too.

I don't know who initiated it, but in the glow of the television, Lilith and I were kissing. We were full-on making out like two horny middle schoolers that have never kissed before. Tongues and hands were exploring. Images of what could happen next were racing through my mind. I was not even sure I wanted what could happen next. I was just lost in that particular moment.

"I knew it!" my mother screeched with glee from her couch. This broke the moment. I could not let my mother think she was right about anything when it came to me and my life.

I stood up, throwing Lilith to the floor.

"Get the fuck away from me," I growled, fists clenched at my side.

Lilith looked up at me. For a minute she looked sad, heartbroken almost. But then she grinned and shrugged. That's how it always was with her. She never cowered. She never became pathetic.

She pulled herself up off the floor in a drunken, clumsy manner. She let out a big, tired sigh and then unexpectedly let her hand fly out. I caught her smack with my face.

"You show him, Lilith!" my mother laughed, instigating her.

Now I was beyond pissed. I grabbed Lilith by her shoulders and swung her around and up against the wall unit.

"Did you just fuckin' hit me, bitch?" I asked. It was a stupid question, but I was drunk out of my mind.

"You are a fuckin' bastard, Heck."

I took her and slammed her again. I didn't mean for it to be too hard. I just wanted to scare her, but my drunken enraged mind got the best of me.

She gasped, having the wind knocked out of her. Her grin fell from her face, and I could see she was struggling to contain her own drunken thoughts. Before I knew what was happening, her knee came up and rammed me right in the crotch.

I roared with pain and fell to my knees with my hands on my crotch. Stars of pain shot everywhere. I gulped down the vomit I could feel slowly making its way up my chest. I could hear her giggling.

"Know this, Heck," she said, standing with a slight sway in her posture, "I always get the last say. Always!"

She walked away, grabbed her things, and left the house, slamming the door behind her. She left me howling in pain and rage while my mother laughed like she had just witnessed the funniest thing she ever saw.

The fog cleared. I was still in front of the park, the radio on. The Metallica song was long gone, and it was time for the weather and news. Weirdly, I could feel the phantom pain in my crotch.

I rubbed my eyes to clear the lingering green, fuzzy spots in my vision, then set myself up for another round of coke. I had barely remembered that night, we were so fucked up, but I did remember the next morning. I had found Lilith crashed in the back of her van in my driveway. She woke up, just as hungover as I was. We went about our morning as if nothing had happened. That was how it usually was with us.

I spotted some kids in the park, cutting class, and was happy to see that one of them was Bo, Lilith's little brother. He was a skinny little punk in jeans and an olive-green flight jacket. He was casually standing with some buddies, joking around. It must have been something funny because one of his friends was patting him on the back in a good-natured way.

I exited the car and made my way up the concrete path towards him. He spotted me immediately and his whole demeanor changed. He stood straight up, chest puffed and arms threateningly to his sides. His head was held high as he said something I could not hear. But whatever he said, his friends took the same stance around him. All of them watched me as I approached them, looking at me like they were ready to jump my ass.

"Hey, Bo," I called out. You could hear the nervousness in my voice.

"Don't come any closer, Asshole!"

I stopped. Lilith's family was taking our falling out so seriously. In their defense, they kind of had a right to, but I was one hundred percent positive she made it worse than it needed to be. God only knew what she filled their heads with when it came to us.

"Come on, Bo," I said. "I just want to talk about Lilith—"

"You keep my sister's name out of your fuckin' mouth!" he screamed. "You don't get to say her name. You don't get to talk about her. Ever again!"

Two of his friends began to step forward toward me. I took a step back.

"Just get the fuck out of here, man," one of them said.

"You don't understand…" I said, putting my hands up and walking backward. "I just need Bo for a minute."

"Either leave or stay and find out what happens," the other friend said as more of Bo's friends began to approach me.

That was my cue. I was not stupid. There were more of them than me. And some of them were big kids too. If they jumped me, it would be game over for me. They would put me out of commission, and it would be a one-way ticket to hell from there.

I went back to the car feeling furious and frustrated. I was getting so tired of these games that Lilith loved to play. It was always Lilith that knew just how to push my buttons. I wondered, briefly, if I could get away with killing her after she forgave me. Send her to her own damnation. I imagined I was grabbing her by the throat and squeezing the life out of her. Her eyes would bulge, and her tongue would swell. She would claw at me in a desperate attempt to make me stop. She was smart enough to get some of my skin under her nails so I could be identified as her killer. The joke would be on her, though, because after I crushed her last breath out of her and after her heart ceased beating its final beat, I would just lay down beside her and let death come for me. Our corpses would be found side by side, like some dark and twisted Romeo and Juliet.

I had to think. All of Lilith's siblings shot me down. Her mother slammed the door in my face. There was Heather, but I pretty much promised to leave her alone. I tucked Heather in my back pocket as a last resort.

I was tired and getting hungry again. My head was a whirlwind of emotions, and I was beginning to feel as if I was going to crack. Maybe I should just give up. If hell was my most miserable on earth, would it be that bad? I was miserable all the time, anyway. What difference would it make?

I could not let Destiny win, though. I had to find Lilith and prove that not only would Lilith forgive me, but she would love me.

The idea of the library popped into my head. Lilith was often found there to use their reference books for her bootleg papers. There was a very good chance I would find her there.

I had to drive two towns over because Garden Hollows was too shitty of a town to have a proper library. God forbid we should encourage learning something more than how to break a law or mix a fine drink for mommy.

I looked for Lilith's unmistakable white van in the library parking lot but did not see it. Maybe she did not even have it anymore. Last I heard, it was run down and giving her trouble. She might have trashed it for something newer in the past year.

I walked into the library and could feel the ladies staring at me. I was not exactly the type of person one would find in a library. Neither was Lilith for the most part, but that just went to show that you could not judge a book by its cover.

I looked up and down the rows of shelves that housed thousands of books. I checked the tables where a couple of students and some older folks were sitting quietly, reading or researching. There was no sign of her.

There was still a good chance she could walk in, so I decided to stay and hang out with the hopes of bumping into her. I browsed the spines of the books to find something to read so I would look more inconspicuous. I found a section on faith and spirituality and grabbed a book on angels and demons.

Sitting across from an old man with a nasty smoker's cough, I thumbed through the book with some interest. Nowhere did it mention what I was going through. There was no mention of a beautiful dark angel with a shit-eating grin whose main purpose was to make the end of my life miserable.

I suddenly had a scary thought. What if this was my hell? Just an eternity of trying to find Lilith, and Destiny taunting me. What if I was already dead and this was my hell? What if Saturday's midnight never came? I just go round and round, looking for Lilith forever and ever? For all of time's eternity?

The thought made me shudder. No, I had to find Lilith. I had to get that forgiveness and make it through the pearly gates that were illustrated in the book I was scanning.

The fog was coming again. I did not even bother fighting it. Truth was, it killed time and took me away from the hell I was going through here, even though it was sending me to a past hell.

I had just finished my shift and Lilith picked me up. It was our usual routine to either head to my house or her house so I could shower and clean up. On this particular day, we chose her house.

I kept extra clothes there; a couple of pairs of jeans, underwear, and two shirts. They were always waiting for me, perfectly laundered and folded. I did not know if it was Lilith who washed them or her mother. I never thought to ask. It was just nice to have that little act of kindness done for me.

The house was crawling with people hanging out, as usual. Bo and his buddies were outside messing around with one of the cars that always seemed to be parked on Patton's property. Verona was in the living room with some kids watching real people living with real problems on MTV. Lilith's mother was cooking up something inexpensive but filling in the kitchen that smelled warm and comforting.

"Hey Mom," I greeted as Lilith and I headed upstairs. "Smells amazing."

"Wash up. It'll be ready in twenty," she called up after us.

Most people would find what Lilith and I did next odd, but for us, it was perfectly normal. I would jump in the shower and close the curtain. Then she would come into the bathroom and sit on the floor. We would hang out and talk. We would talk about our day and plan our evening. We would gossip about the neighborhood gossip and decide which of our friends was getting on our nerves and why. I don't know how this habit began or when, but it was a part of who we were. There was no privacy or boundaries between us.

I turned off the shower and reached my hand out beyond the blue shower curtain. She handed me a towel which I wrapped around my waist before pulling the plastic curtain aside. She looked up at me from her spot on the floor and smiled, raising her eyebrows.

"Looking sexy there, Heck," she joked.

"Whatever," I grumbled. "Get out. Gotta dress."

The memory was quick and faded away in a blink. I was back in the library. I don't even know why I was shown that memory. It seemed pretty useless to me. It was just a blip in the relationship between Lilith and me. It was one of many days, of many moments that Lilith and I spent together. Maybe the memory was meant to show me how nice our friendship could be or how intimate it was but, truthfully, I did not care. I wanted these flashbacks to stop wasting my time. More than likely, it was Destiny messing with me.

I looked around the library, almost positive that Destiny was going to show her grinning face in the form of a sexy librarian or something. But she never showed. She did say she was going to leave me alone. Maybe she was true to her word, though I doubt it. I did not trust anyone, let alone the devil. If that was what she was.

I pondered on that. Was she the devil? Her grin was certainly filled with hate and evil. Or maybe she was the grim reaper? Was it possible she was a guardian angel, using scare tactics to show me the way?

I did not even know anymore. I was so tired. I was at the point where I just wanted everything over with. Lying down for eternal sleep was starting to sound good to me. I would welcome a nice, long dirt nap at this point.

It was dark outside, and the library was beginning to close up. Lilith never showed, so that was a waste of time. Precious time too.

I was done. I still had time. Not much, but I never wanted to crash and burn like I did at that very moment. I needed to go home and just hit my bed. I settled on the fact that I would just have to go back to Heather and Mitch and beg them for Lilith's whereabouts. They would give in. I knew that.

At home, I was once again screamed at by Freddie for taking his car and keeping it for two days. I was screamed at by my mother for reasons I could not even wrap my brain around. I did not even scream back. The walls were not punched. The doors were not slammed. I just walked past them and went straight to my room, locking the door behind me.

I set my alarm for the morning. I would have all day to find Lilith. It was my final day, but my last day would belong entirely to Lilith. That irony was not lost on me.

My sleep was deep but filled with dreams. So many memories were flooding my slumber. From my early childhood with my grandmother, who was long gone, to my early teens with my father just before he was arrested and sent away. There were rare moments of my mother being halfway decent in some of our most disturbing fights. There were concerts I attended and parties I crashed. Laws I had broken and fights and tears I had caused. There was stupid, stoner laughter and manic, wired discussions.

I could hear Ugly Kid Joe's "I Hate Everything About You" playing somewhere in the distance. It was getting louder and louder, echoing in my brain and washing away the dreams.

It was my clock radio, blaring away. Groaning, I reached over to turn the alarm off. I bolted up when I saw the time. 2:12. It was way after noon. I overslept.

I was in such a deep sleep that I had slept through over seven hours of my clock radio blasting music, news, weather, and commercials.

It had to be on purpose. This had to be Destiny's doing. She knew I was getting close to finding Lilith. She had to have known my plan. She had to know that Heather would give me what I was looking for.

I threw on my clothes and rushed out of the house. Freddie's car was gone and there was no way my mother would let me take hers. I wasn't going to waste time fighting with her for her keys. I had no choice but to walk. I could have called a cab, but who knew how long it would take to show up? I would get to Mitch's house quicker on foot.

I walked quickly, head down and fists rammed in my jacket pockets. The air was chilly, and the leaves were golden and crunched under my boots. It was the perfect fall afternoon. My nose was beginning to run from the crisp, cold air and shockingly not from overuse of blow.

I made it to Mitch's house in record time with my chest heaving with shortness of breath. I was so unhealthy. Never mind the drugs and drinking. Smoking since I was 12 years old was enough to render me incapable of walking at a quick pace for over a mile.

Or maybe it was not the walking and shitty lungs. Maybe this is how I die. Time just slowly squeezing the air out of me.

I knocked on the door, then stepped back to light up a cigarette. I was expecting Mitch to answer and have to put up a fight to speak to Heather, but I was surprised to see her answering the door. I was even more surprised that she did not seem surprised to see me standing there.

"They told me you would be coming," she said through the screen door, arms folded across her chest.

"Who?" I was confused. Did Destiny tell her or something?

"My cousins."

"Oh. You heard from Lilith then," I said, getting excited.

She looked at me strangely, then sighed with defeat.

"No, dummy. Morella. Verona. They told me you were looking for Lilith and you were most likely going to hit me up next," she explained.

"Oh."

I just stood there, feeling lost and stupid. I was at a loss for words because I just assumed she would tell me either where to find Lilith or to go fuck myself. She just stared at me; eyes squinted with disgust.

"Holy fuck, Heather!" I finally snapped. "Can you please tell me where I can find Lilith? I'm begging you here!"

"No. I won't do that to her."

"Do what? It's what she would want. She would want me to go to her and tell her how sorry I am and what a dick I am. Jesus Christ, she would love that! She would be in her glory to have me crawling to her!"

"I don't think you realize how much she hated you," Heather said.

"And I don't think you realize how much she loves me!"

Again, a silence came between us. I could see a shadow moving behind her and it turned out to be Mitch. He walked closer until I could see him clearly. I breathed out a huff. I did not need him to tell me to get bent. Not now. I needed to find Lilith. Heather was my last hope.

Instead, Mitch reached around Heather and opened the door. He stuck his hand out with a piece of paper in it.

"Mitch, no," Heather whined with that mousy voice of hers.

"No. Let him go find her. He deserves whatever he's got coming," Mitch laughed, handing me the paper.

It had an address scribbled on it. My heart never jumped from excitement and then slammed down in despair as fast as it did when I read the address. I felt sick.

8416 D Row

St. Michael's Drive

San Elmo, California

"California? She's in California?" It was my turn to have a squeaky voice. That was a long way from Garden Hollows. Too long, by my quick calculations.

"She moved there a couple of months ago," she said. I detected a hint of sadness in her voice. I guessed she was missing her, but not as much as I was right then and there.

"I don't need to see her," I said. "I just need her number. I just need her phone number. I can call her. I just need to talk to her."

I was beyond desperate now. I was frantic.

Mitch laughed, pulling the screen door shut between us.

"Good luck with that, Dick!"

The door slammed shut.

I was alone on their stoop, freezing, winded, and with nothing but a useless address in my hand. I was lost.

California was across the country. Lilith was across the country. My final fate was across the country. My mind whirled into confusion and defeat.

I walked away from Mitch's house in a bewildered state. I did not know what to do or where to go. I did not even know where I was walking until I was just blocks from my house.

My mother was passed out on the couch. I tried to think. I could call an airline and see if there were any flights or how long a flight was. I knew nothing about flying. I had never been on a plane before. But I knew it could not hurt to at least call and find out some information. Either way, I was a dead man.

Questions were asked and I was somewhat pleased with the answers. Yes, there were flights to the airport nearest to San Elmo. The flight was five hours, but then that would mean I would get there close to midnight. That was cutting it way too close. But then the operator told me the sweetest news I had had all week.

"No. You misunderstand," she said, "There's a time difference. You would be landing at 9 pm."

My mind reeled from this information. Could I cheat death and gain three hours just by flying across the country? I had to try. Worse came to worse, I died on the plane. At least I would die doing something I had never done before.

I grabbed my mother's purse and took her wallet. I rummaged through it and found her credit cards. The flight was booked.

I had very little time. I immediately called for a cab to take me to the airport. I didn't even pack. Why would I? I was only flying one way. From home to California to die at Lilith's doorstep.

I waited in the living room, lighting up a smoke nervously. Funny how flying was making me nervous, but death was not. And yet the whole reason why I was nervous about flying was that we could crash and end in death. If we crashed, I would never get that forgiveness from Lilith. It would be straight to whatever hell was waiting for me.

I looked down at my mother, her chest raising and lowering from a deep, drunken slumber. Loud snores kept getting trapped somewhere between the back of her throat and her nose. I wondered how long it would be before she realized I have not been home in weeks. I assumed Lilith would call her with the news that I was no longer of the earth. Would my mother pay to have my body flown home? Or would she just tell Lilith to put my cold corpse to the curb in a trash bag like the garbage I was? I wondered, more than anything, if my mother would cry for me. Would she mourn the death of her firstborn son? Or would she be relieved that she no longer had to feel some sort of responsibility for me?

A car honked, the driver signaling his arrival. I took one last look at my mother and then just left. No kiss. No goodbye. Nothing. I felt nothing toward that moment.

I approached the cab, which was nothing but a run-down, beat-up, sky-blue Impala, half expecting Destiny to be at the steering wheel. Part of me was relieved that it was an old man. There was also a part of me who realized I would have found comfort in Destiny driving me to the airport.

There was no traffic, and the drive seemed to be moving along swiftly, but the clock ticking down felt faster. My chest hurt as I struggled to take that occasional deep breath. I ignored the invisible clamp around my ribs, back, and chest as a haze fell over me. For some reason, I knew where this memory trip was going. There were only so many days left in Lilith's and my friendship. And those days were not good ones.

I tried to pull away from the fog and bring myself back to the cab whizzing down the highway. I did not want to relive this memory. No one wants to relive a night of regret.

The magical hold was too strong, though. I came out of the shadows and fog and found myself drunk and sweaty in Garden Hollows' crappy little playground.

It was a hot summer night. One of those nights where no one was going to get any sleep. It was the kind of heat that made people irrational and do crazy and impulsive things.

We all chose to hang out in the dead of night at the playground. We were too old to be at the playground, but it was cheaper than one of the dive bars. Cops never cared when we chose to drink and loiter. No one cared in Garden Hollows.

Lilith and I were trashed, along with everyone else. We had some poor sap trapped on a park bench as we teased and argued with him. It did not even matter what the conversation was about. He caught our eye or ear, and we were now standing over him, drunkenly pointing at him, and ragging into him. We were loud. We were obnoxious. And we were annoying the shit out of everyone around us.

"Jesus Christ!" Mitch shouted from his spot on a swing. "Can you two just quit it? Take it home!"

"Oh, fuck you!" I yelled back as Lilith laughed.

"Seriously, Lilith, just go home. Take him with you," Freddie chimed in. "Enough is enough. No one cares tonight. Either shut up and chill or go home."

Lilith's smile fell from her face. I could see the spark in her eyes as she rushed to my brother and got in his face.

"Really, Freddie? You gonna start with me too?"

"Whoa!" I said, pulling her away from him.

"You two are assholes," Freddie mumbled, stepping away from us.

"What the fuck did we do?" I screeched, totally lost to how this fight started. Then again, I was usually lost to how fights started.

"Lilith, just take him home!" Mitch screamed.

"Fuck this shit," Lilith said, pulling on my arm. "They don't want us, then fuck them."

She pulled me out of the park, neither one of us capable of walking a straight line. I could hear Mitch comment about Lilith and me deserving each other. It made my skin itch.

"Fuck them," Lilith repeated with a giggle, "We can still hang."

I looked down and saw she had a bottle of whatever fruit-infused brandy we were drinking still in her hand. I laughed, grabbing it from her and taking a swig.

The walk back to her house was slow because of the heat, and the fact that we were two drunken fools. We spent the whole time bitching about all of our friends. It was irking me that my brother was the one who told us to leave.

"Freddie kicking us out…who the hell does he think he is?" I slurred as we walked into her house. Her sisters were still awake, sitting on the couch. They were trying to keep cool with loud, old box fans. The only light on came from the television where an old, late-night rerun of The Honeymooners was on.

"Eh, he was stoned off his ass. He don't know what he's saying," Lilith said.

"You taking his side? He started it with you."

Lilith shrugged as she kicked her sneakers off.

"What the fuck, Lilith. How does this not piss you off?"

Her sisters shot each other a knowing glance. They could see a fight starting to brew between Lilith and me. They knew the signs. They have witnessed it many times before.

"Heck," she sighed, "I'm going upstairs. I'm gonna smoke up a little, put on some music and I'm gonna zone. You can join me or sit with my sisters. Or you can go home to Freddie and your mommy. I don't give a shit."

I stared at her in disbelief as she climbed the stairs. It was not what she said, but rather how she said it. She knew being so nonchalant would get me going even more. She knew what she was doing, especially calling my mother *mommy*. She knew that would piss me off. I should have walked away and found somewhere else to crash. Anywhere else.

But instead, I chose to follow her and engage.

"I don't need you ragging on me too!" I hissed, closing her bedroom door behind us. "I get it already from everyone else. Everyone is always dissing me! I didn't need it from Freddie and I sure as fuck don't need it from you!"

"Everyone disses you because you are an asshole, Heck!"

"I'm an asshole? Why am I an asshole?"

"Yes! Because you are too stupid to see what you've got!" she screamed.

"What do I have, Lilith? Tell me! What do I have? I live in a piss poor town that I am never gonna get out of. I have a shitty job. My brother is a loser. My mother is a drunk. I'm a junkie," I yelled. "Tell me! What the fuck do I have?"

"You have me!"

And there it was. An old fight coming to the surface again.

"Don't start this shit again," I mumbled, running my hand through my hair and pushing it back.

"Why? It's the truth! Here I am, Heck! I have been here for a long time now!"

"We are just friends!"

"Are we? Let's be real about this!" she continued, her finger pointing at me. "We do everything together. If you are not at work and if I'm not working on a paper, we are together. I make sure you are fed. I make sure you get to work on time. I even make sure your mother is taken care of half the time! Let's face it, Heck! We are practically married!!"

"Fuck no!"

"No? No? How is it no? The only difference between us and a married couple is that we don't fuck! And I don't know why. Why can't I be the one for you? I don't even know why I want to be the one for you. You are nothing."

"Lilith," I growled. My head was beginning to spin. My fists were clenched at my sides, my jaw set.

"You are nothing but a dirty, filthy, no good, low class, white trash, uneducated, drug addicted—"

"Shut up," I warned her.

"Liar, user, cheater, punk-ass, thief, scuzzbucket, dirtbag—", she continued, getting louder with each word.

"I'm warning you," I hissed.

"Asshole, son-of-a-goddamn-no-good-motherfuckin-bitch! Bastard! You will burn in hell for eternity!" she roared, stepping closer to me and standing right in front of my face.

"Bitch!" I yelled, grabbing her by her shirt with one hand and raising my other hand in a fist.

Her face softened. She didn't flinch. Not even a wince. Instead, she smiled.

"But I love you, anyway."

That was Lilith. She was just like me. There was something dark and ugly inside of her. She knew that rage and she embraced it. Just like me.

We stood there, almost panting, staring at one another. I had never felt such intensity. I wanted to pound my fist into her face and wreck her smile. I wanted to take her and shake her like a rag doll to knock some sense into her and force her to realize we would never be what she wanted us to be.

Instead, my poised fist relaxed. I reached down and touched her cheek, my thumb trailing her lips. She let out a loud sigh. I still held onto her shirt as I continued to lightly outline and caress her chin and then her neck. My whole hand was around her neck, my thumb on her windpipe and my fingers wrapped around to the back, under her brown hair. I realized that I could easily crush her, but I didn't want that. For the first time, I wanted something physical that wasn't unbridled violence.

"Okay," I said softly, suddenly tightening my grip on both her shirt and her neck. In true Lilith fashion, her eyes gleamed and her smile turned to a grin. Her eyebrows raised in amusement.

I violently threw her down on the bed and fell on top of her. Our teeth clashed as our lips met. I could hear the sounds of cloth tearing and wasn't even sure if it was mine or hers. Our clothes were spent, and our limbs entwined. Nothing was loving or tender between us. It was all physical and raw. It was as if we could not get enough of each other. All our hate and rage were mounting, begging to be released. We were passionate and furious. Being with Lilith was unlike being with any other girl I was with. It was not just sex. But it was not making love either. I did not know what it was, and it scared me and enticed me at the same time.

It ended with our sweaty bodies draped lazily over each other with the heat, drugs, and passion taking over. I drifted off into a deep sleep with confusing dreams that seemed almost feverish. Nothing but clips and flashes of Lilith and me.

I was awake when the sun was rising. This had to be the earliest I had ever been awake in years. I sat up, lit a cigarette, and stared down at Lilith. She seemed to be sleeping peacefully, her arm tucked under her pillow and her hair fanned out.

There was no way we could be together. We were too much alike. I could not be with someone who was just like me. I didn't like myself. How could I love her?

She must have sensed me staring at her because her eyes fluttered open. A smile spread across her face as she rolled onto her back. She reached up and took my cigarette from me to take a drag.

I swung my legs off the bed and grabbed my T-shirt. I held it up, seeing a hole in the seam at the shoulder.

"Sorry about that," she laughed.

"Yeah. No problem."

Standing up, I threw my jeans on. I put the tattered shirt on, not caring about the tear.

"What are you doing?" she asked, sitting up. She knew. She had to know. Her smile was gone. Her brows were knitted.

"I'm out," I said.

"Where are you going? Hang out. I can drive you to work."

"No. No more of this...this..." I tried to find the right words.

"No more with this playing house shit. You are not my wife. You will never be my fuckin' wife!"

Her breath sucked in.

"I need a break," I continued. "I need a break from you. From this. This weird ass friendship we got going? I need a fuckin' break."

"Friendship? I thought we just proved it was more than friendship, Heck."

"Uh-uh. Nope," I shook my head, pulling my boots on. "I don't know what the fuck last night was, but no. Don't let it go to your head. It was a drunken stupid thing. It was nothing."

"If it was nothing, you wouldn't be so bothered," she laughed. Goddamn her and her laugh. Girls are supposed to cry in times like this. Not laugh. She was also telling the truth, but I ignored that.

"Just stop, Lilith!" I screamed. "Get it through your thick fuckin' skull! We will never be together!"

She reached over to an old beer bottle and dropped the cigarette butt into it. Pulling the sheets around her, she sat up and stared at me with a sigh.

"One way or another," she said, "God's gonna see that we end up together."

I looked at her with disbelief. I rolled my eyes and let out a snort of disgust. She was so exhausting that I could not even get mad anymore.

"Why?" I asked. "Why are you so determined?"

"I don't know," she said with a shrug. "You are such a bastard. Yet I'm such a bitch. We are two seriously fucked up people that should hate each other, yet we don't."

"We are going to end up hating each other. You see that coming, don't you?"

"At least we will still have feelings for each other. Love…hate… both such passionate feelings. Sometimes, it's hard to tell the difference."

I stood up and grabbed my pack of smokes. I had to get away from her. I had to make her get away from me. I opened her bedroom door and looked back over at her.

"You are one crazy bitch," I said before walking out.

"I know," she called out after me. *"And you love me, anyway!"*

I was yanked back to the backseat of the cab. We were just pulling up in front of the airport. Lilith's last line was echoing in my head.

"And you love me, anyway!" repeated over and over, rattling in my brain, as I paid the driver, picked up my ticket, and found a seat to wait to board my plane. I should have been overwhelmed, maybe even excited, with the whole plane flying process. It was my first flight. But instead, I was numb. I went through the motions, feeling the tightness around my ribs slowly creeping up to my throat, time closing in on me.

As I sat and waited, my right leg bouncing up and down with anxiety and withdrawal, I tried to people-watch. I tried to breathe as calmly as I could, aware of each inhale and exhale. I began to drift, again, into the foggy haze of months ago.

It was a week or so after that insane night with Lilith. We had been avoiding each other. It was the longest we had ever gone without talking to one another since our friendship began. I could not say I missed her, but there was something thrown off about my days.

I had already started seeing Heather. I wish I could say I chose to start dating Heather because I genuinely liked her and had feelings for her. The truth was, she was just another pawn in my games with Lilith. What better way to prove to Lilith that we were never meant to be than dating her own cousin? And it did not hurt that Heather was easy on the eyes and always eager to impress.

I was on my way home from work when my beeper went off. 666-51-313. It was Lilith. She was using one of the many different codes we had to get messages to one another, so we didn't need to find a payphone. 666 meant she was holding and ready to share and have a good time. 51 was the address of where she was at. In this case, it was the old motor lodge. 313 was the room number.

I sighed, shaking my head. I really didn't want to see her. But at the same time, she scored some lines. She had to know that Heather and I were seeing each other, so maybe everything could go back to normal. She wouldn't put up a scene if I brought Heather along. And maybe some more friends.

That was my plan. It went against our rule of it just being us sharing the blow before friends. But I needed to surround Lilith and me with the usual gang. Maybe it would keep the night from going to hell. I picked up Heather, then swung by my house to find Freddie. The last stop was Mitch. Then, it was a party.

If Lilith was surprised or disappointed that I had our friends with us, she did not let on when she opened the motel door. Not even a flicker of jealousy in her eyes. She just smiled away, back to her usual self. I knew the truth, though. I knew there was an ugly turmoil raging in the pit of her stomach.

I could also tell by the way she was just chattering away about anything and everything, she had started the party without us. Her eyes were huge, and she spoke with her voice slightly high-pitched. I wondered how many lines she already did.

Music played and the air was smoky. The television was on but the sound was muted. Some old 70s movie was playing that no one had any interest in. We settled into our usual conversations. Mostly complaining about Garden Hollows. Talking about getting out even though we knew we would never get out.

Lilith stood by the bathroom door, staring at me. I looked her way and she nodded towards the bathroom. Sighing, I got up and followed her. She shut the door behind us, giving us privacy.

"What's up?" I asked, hoping she wouldn't bring up our last encounter.

She reached deep into her jeans pocket and pulled out a little, crumbled silver gum wrapper. She carefully unfolded it, revealing two small pills.

"I was able to get these," she said excitedly. "I was only able to get two. Want to try?"

"What is it?"

"Supposed to make you zone out. Get you all mellow and shit," she shrugged.

"I don't know—"

"Oh, c'mon, Heck! Let's have a good time. We're friends, right? It's all good," she said, her voice a little shaky.

"Lil, how much you do tonight?"

"I dunno. Who cares? We doing this?"

I looked at her then back down at the pills in her hand. I shook my head. I just wanted to get back out to Heather and continue the night the way it was. Why start something when it was going so well? If it ain't broke, why fix it?

I walked past her and let myself out of the bathroom. I took my place back on one of the two beds in the room, Heather curling up in the crook of my arm. Lilith came out and stared at us for a second.

There it was. I saw it. That glimmer of hate flashed in her eyes. I smiled, knowingly at Lilith, and stroked Heather's hair. Lilith suddenly grinned. She walked to the little table where the white lines were laid out. She picked up the dollar we rolled and used it to snort two lines.

She turned, leaned on the dresser, and continued to stare at me. No one else noticed the quiet little showdown that was going on between us.

She pinched her nose and sniffed. I kissed Heather's neck, my eyes never leaving Lilith. She swigged on her beer. I stroked Heather's thigh, letting my hand wander past her skirt's hem. Lilith's hand reached up and I saw her pop her pill in her mouth. Maybe she popped both of them. I didn't care. I turned Heather's face to mine to kiss her. My eyes never left Lilith. Lilith took another gulp of her beer to wash it down. Finally, she turned away to talk to Mitch and Freddie. I won.

I don't know how much time had passed, how many songs had played, or how many lines were snorted, but the atmosphere changed in the dimly lit motel room. We realized Lilith's fast-paced talking had ceased and she had been sitting in a chair, quietly. Her eyes were so glassy they looked as if they were filled with tears. Mitch was talking to her, but she looked like she couldn't find the words to talk. And I did not care.

I got up to go to the bathroom while Heather and Freddie tried talking to Lilith. I could hear Heather's voice getting squeaky with panic when I came back out. They were all surrounding Lilith, who just continued to gaze around the room silently. It was eerie.

"Dude, something's wrong with her," Mitch called out to me.

"She's fine. She took some pills. She'll ride it out," I said, sitting on the edge of the bed and lighting a cigarette.

"What? What did she take?"

"I dunno," I shrugged.

Lilith suddenly started to make a weird little gasping noise and her breath became jagged and hard.

"What the fuck?" Freddie yelled, jumping away from her. Heather reached out, grabbing her wrist.

"Oh my god! Her heart is racing!"

"She's crashing," Mitch said.

"Just give her some weed. It'll slow her down," I said, annoyed. This was what Lilith wanted. She wanted us to panic. She wanted me to become concerned for her. It wasn't working. Not this time.

"We have to call 911," Heather said on the verge of crying.

"Are you nuts?" I yelled. "We'll get thrown in jail. I'm not going to jail for her crazy ass! She's the one that bought the blow! She's the one that took God knows what!"

Everyone looked at me in disbelief. How was this suddenly my fault?

"Fuck!" I screamed, throwing my beer bottle against the wall. I paced the short floor for only a couple of seconds, trying to think.

"Heck, we need—" Mitch started, but I cut him off.

"Just get her ass in my car," I groaned. "I'll take her to the ER."

I swear, Lilith lifted her glazed eyes at me and sneered. Even in her state, she was still playing the game. One of those days, I was really going to hit her.

"Just grab her and get her down to my car, let's go!" I ordered. "Or I'm just going home and leaving all of you to deal with her bullshit."

I walked out, leaving them to figure out how to get her down the stairs and to the parking lot. I didn't even know why I was volunteering to do this. I should have just left her there to die.

Mitch and Freddie half dragged/half carried Lilith down with Heather now full-blown sobbing behind them. They stuffed her in the passenger seat while I got behind the wheel. As soon as her door was closed, I took off. I didn't even bother to see if she was comfortable.

Lilith's breathing was quick and short. I had to admit she did not look good. I could see that death was slowly inching towards her and if she did not get medical help, death would win. As I drove towards the hospital, the road nothing but fields on both sides, I wondered what would happen if I pulled over and did nothing. Just dump her in a field.

It was so tempting. Her crazy ass would be out of my life for good. I looked over at her. She looked pathetic, breathing like an asthmatic, her eyes all buggy. She smiled at me as if she knew what I was thinking.

"I should," I mumbled. "I should just leave you here. Forget about you for good."

"You…won't," she whispered.

The flashback broke back to the airport. My flight was being called. It was my time to board the plane. A one-way ticket to California. A one-way ticket to my eternity. Heaven or Hell, whatever Lilith decides. I shook my head with disbelief that my fate lay entirely in Lilith's hands, and she did not even know.

I boarded the plane, looking for Destiny. I thought she would be a flight attendant or maybe a passenger sitting next to me, but she was nowhere to be seen. I wondered if I would ever see her again before meeting my demise.

I found flying to be just like on television and in the movies. They gave the whole safety spiel and the captain announced that the weather was looking good, and we should be getting to our destination in good time. The seats were small and stuffy, but the person next to me left me alone.

I gazed out the window as we pulled up into the dark sky. I felt like I should have been saying some sort of symbolic goodbye to Garden Hollows, but I didn't. That town and its people never did me any good, anyway. At least I was getting out. I was not going to die in that miserable shit hole. That was more than most people could say.

The drink cart made its round, and I could feel the fingers of death getting tighter around my throat with each mile we flew. I felt sweaty and lightheaded. Excusing myself and climbing past my seat mates, I made my way to the bathroom. I locked myself in, splashing water on my face. I looked in the mirror and was shocked to see how sickly I looked. I looked deranged with the wounds from the accident slowly healing and my skin grey. My eyes were sunken and ringed with stress.

I saw some darkness peeking around my collar and pulled my shirt down to see a webbing of black.

"What the fuck?" I lifted my shirt to see my chest was covered with this black, splattered-looking bruise. It was trailing up my neck and shoulders. It laced down my stomach, disappearing behind the waistband of my jeans. This was not normal bruising caused by a physical impact on my skin. This was something dark and grotesque manifesting from somewhere deep within me. It hurt my eyes to even look at it. I tried to think what it could be. Maybe the hospital missed some internal bleeding. Or maybe it was death eating away at me from the inside.

I held onto the tiny sink to keep from swaying. I was feeling unsteady, and it was not because of the flight. The fog was coming again. This was getting so tiring. I figured my memories with Lilith would be the most tiresome.

I didn't leave a dying, overdosing Lilith on the side of the road. I couldn't. I did leave her outside the ER, though. Pulled in, pulled her out of the car, dropped her on the ground, and drove off. I left her to be someone else's problem. I was not about to stick around answering questions about who she was, who she was to me, and all her drug history. She was the hospital's problem.

It was three days later when I received word that Lilith wanted to see me. I didn't want to go, but Heather insisted. I let myself be talked into visiting her at the hospital.

I walked into Lilith's room, braced for a shouting match about me leaving her. I was surprised to see her just laying there with an almost content look on her face.

"Didn't think you'd come," she smiled weakly.

"Didn't want to," I admitted.

"Fair enough."

I stood there, an awkward pause lingering in the air. The weird hospital noises were getting to me. The machines monotonously let out an occasional beep. There was a whooshing sound that you always heard in hospitals but never knew what it was. It was quiet but loud all at the same time.

"I'm getting out," she finally said, a note of sadness in her voice.

"Yeah? They letting you go?"

"That's not what I mean. I mean, I'm getting out of this…this shitty life. No more drugs for me. I'm going clean."

"Yeah, right," I laughed.

"No. I mean it, Heck. They said my lungs are deteriorating. There is so much damage done to my liver…" she trailed off, looking at her hands. "I died, Heck. They had to bring me back."

"Alright. Cool." I didn't know what else to say. I didn't know what she wanted from me.

"Do it with me," Lilith whispered, almost begging. "Go clean with me."

"Seriously?" I laughed.

"We belong together. We can do this together."

"And there it is! Enough! I can't anymore, Lil! It's over! There never was an us!"

"Heck—"

"NO! No more," I roared. I didn't care if I was in a hospital. I was not keeping my cool. I was not letting her have the final say. "You need to get it through your thick, delusional, fuckin' skull that there is no us!"

"Oh, there will always be an us," she laughed, even though tears streamed down her cheeks.

"I'm with Heather now! She's gonna move in with me."

"You're not gonna last," she said. She was teasing me. Mocking, even. And she seemed so spiteful.

"Fuck you! You are just the same jealous little bitch you always were."

"You'll break up. You always do. It didn't take much for me to break you and Melissa up. It will take even less for me to break you and Heather up."

I squinted at her, confusion overcoming me. She laughed.

"Oh, come on Heck. You're dumb, but you're not that dumb. Think about it," she continued. "All the times I told you Melissa was cheating on you…all the times I let Melissa think you were cheating on her…I may have even implied we were more than just friends. That was not a hard one for her to believe."

I backed away from her bed. She was beyond crazy.

"You fuckin' bitch."

She just shrugged. She didn't care.

"I should have left you on the side of the road!"

"But you didn't."

"Burn in hell!" I screamed. "Die and rot!"

"I probably will. But you're gonna go down with me."

Someone knocked on the bathroom door of the airplane. I wondered how long I was gone with that memory. I gathered myself together and exited the tiny closet of a bathroom.

Lilith wasn't wrong. If what Destiny said was true, and Heaven is being with the things that made you happy and hell was being with the things that made you miserable, Lilith would be my hell. The irony of Lilith's forgiveness being my Heaven was very obvious to me.

I was so tired. Exhausted did not even describe what I felt. I was tired of Lilith. Tired of Destiny. And most importantly, tired of myself. I wanted this to be over. The plane could not land fast enough.

The rest of the flight was uneventful. Slow, but no more flashbacks. I prayed that was the end to Lilith's and my tumultuous history. I just wanted to get to her doorstep, get her blessing, and die. I honestly could not think of a better way to get the final say than dropping dead on that obsessive bitch's doorstep. She would have to live with that forever. That was the one silver lining in this dark cloud of death, and it was a beautiful one.

The plane finally landed. The passengers could not grab their bags from the overhead bin and file out fast enough for me. I rushed through the airport with the clock ticking down. I had gained time. It had worked, crossing the time zones. But I only had three hours to spare. Three hours to get to Lilith's home, give my speech, get her forgiveness, and die peacefully. That was a tall order for three measly hours.

I jumped into the first cab I saw and handed the driver the piece of paper with Lilith's address on it.

"How far is it to San Elmo's?" I asked.

"About 30-45 minutes. Closer to an hour with traffic, though. Give or take. Look, this isn't—"

"Just get me there as fast as you can," I said, cutting him off and thrusting two one-hundred-dollar bills in his face. "And please, no talking."

The driver grunted with a roll of his eyes, but he took the money. I settled back in my seat, looking out the window. It was too dark to take in any sights. For the first time I was out of Garden Hollows, far from my home, and I could not even see any of it. Not even from the window of my cab.

The haze came again. At this point, I welcomed it. It had to be my last one. Death was at hand.

It was months since the whole Lilith debacle incident. It was over. She never contacted me, and I never contacted her. The only times we saw each other were when we were together with friends or in a bar. Nine times out of ten that ended with us screaming at each other. The only time we were halfway decent to each other was the night I found out Heather was pregnant.

I was sitting outside with Freddie and some other friends, doing our usual drinking and smoking up. Lilith came walking down my street with her sister, Morella. They were dressed like they were either heading to or heading home from a bar. It did not matter. What did matter was she chose my block to walk down. And I knew it was on purpose.

"You couldn't go another way?" I yelled. "Had to come walking down this way?"

"Free world, Hector!" she yelled back as she walked past me.

"Heather left me for good!" I screamed as I grabbed her arm and spun her to face me.

"I know."

She smiled. And I finally broke. All those years of threatening and clenching my fists. All those times I punched a hole in the wall instead of her or any other woman that drove me to a blind rage, I finally let my fist fly.

I heard my friends gasp, and Morella scream. I heard my knuckles making contact with Lilith's evil, bitchy sneer of a smile. I heard Lilith's body slam down on the cold, hard concrete with a thud. And I heard her as she continued to laugh. I could not even punch that fuckin' smile off her face. She was nothing but pure evil looking up at me with a bloodied grin.

Freddie had to pull me away before I continued to pummel her. Morella helped her up, trying to wipe the blood off of her face with the sleeve of her sweater.

"Let it go!" Freddie said, pushing me towards the house. "Don't make it worse."

"I'm gonna kill her! I swear to God, I'm gonna put her down like the bitch she is!"

"Stop! This is what she wants!" Freddie said.

Lilith didn't even bother continuing fighting with me. She walked away with her sister, disappearing down the street. Her laughter trailed off into the night.

My friends and Freddie calmed me down, handing me a beer and joking about how she had it coming. It was not even half an hour later when we heard the sirens. Flashing blue and red lights immediately followed. The fuckin' bitch called the cops. You did not get any lower than that. It was such a bullshit move on her part and she knew it.

Lilith had pressed assault charges. I ended up spending two nights in jail before appearing before a judge and then being sent off to a month in rehab. And I never saw Lilith again.

The fog cleared. I looked out of my window, confused. Why was my driver cutting through a cemetery? Both sides of the road were lined with a waist-high stone wall that was topped with a towering iron fence. The car came to a slow stop.

"This is it," he said. I looked out the window again, in case I was missing something. There was nothing but gravestone after gravestone.

"What the fuck is this?" I asked.

"This is where you said you wanted to go."

"No, I need to go to a house. I don't have time for this bullshit. I have to see my friend..."

"You gave me a plot location. It's a gravesite number."

"I'm confused. That can't be."

"The address you gave me isn't an address. It's Saint Michael's Cemetery. That's a plot number," he said, pointing to the paper I had handed him earlier. "This is a community cemetery. Where they bury the John Does and the poor. People who don't got anyone to claim them. Folks whose families can't afford a lavish send-off."

"No. No, no, no..."

My head was spinning. Was this a sick joke? Were Mitch and Heather just playing with me? Was it Destiny playing with me? Was I being sent to my own grave to die? A place where no one would claim my corpse?

"I think you should get out," the cab driver said. "You're high or something."

I laughed. For the first time in a long time, I was stone-cold sober. And I was about to be stone-cold dead.

"Let me just think."

"No. You need to get out of my car. Don't make me radio in the police."

That made me move. I had no time to waste. No time at all.

I stood on the street alone, confused, panicked, and surrounded by the dead. There was nothing left for me. No Lilith. Not even Destiny. I couldn't do anything but stare through the slots of the iron gate. It was locked up, no way in. Grabbing the bars, I rested my head on the steel. I was defeated. This was nothing more than a joke. My entire life was a joke and now my death was too.

I heard footsteps in the distance, down the road. I looked up to see a shadow of a woman walking away from me. I squinted to make it out in the moonlight.

"Destiny?" I called out. The shadow looked quickly over her shoulder but kept walking away from me. Her pace quickened.

I followed her, calling out for her again. She did not stop. I followed her, my breath getting even tighter in my chest.

"Please," I said. "Wait…"

No matter how fast I walked, she always seemed ahead, her shadow just barely out of sight. Then she stopped. I blinked and she was gone.

"The fuck," I almost cried. She was torturing me.

I caught up to the spot where she disappeared, catching my breath. I looked around and realized the iron bars in this spot were bent. It was bent with enough room for me to climb through it. I was able to get into the closed cemetery.

I walked among the rows of the dead. Most of the graves had small markers. Some had modest headstones that their families could barely afford. I called out Destiny's name, but she never appeared.

My breathing was getting harder. My lungs felt like they were slowly filling up with fluid. I was drowning.

I stumbled over a newly dug grave and fell to the ground. Lifting my head, I saw the marker. Her name screamed out at me.

Lilith Patton

November 2nd, 1993

"What the fuck?"

I scrambled away from the grave and stood up. She was dead. Lilith was dead all this time. And she died the same day as my accident. Nothing about this made sense anymore.

"Heck?"

I whipped around and saw someone approaching me. A woman walking out of the darkness and into the moonlight. I thought for sure it had to be Destiny, taking me to eternal hell, but I was wrong. It was her. It was Lilith, standing before me. Smiling.

It was all a joke. She was in on it too. Her, her mom, her sisters, Heather, Mitch…it was all an elaborate prank. It had to be. That was the only reasonable explanation, and I did not care. I was just so grateful to see her right in front of me.

Somewhere in the distance, a bell rang. The cemetery's chapel was chiming in, letting me know midnight had finally approached.

"Lilith!" I said, wheezing with each breath. "I don't have time. Please forgive me. Let me die in peace."

The bells chimed again. She walked closer to me and took my hands in hers. She looked so happy. So healthy. So at peace. California seemed good for her.

I could feel my consciousness beginning to slip. The bells continued to chime, counting down the final seconds of my life.

"Please, Lil…"

"No."

And with that, the final chime rang. I looked down at the grave and could see my own body lying there, crumpled in a heap. Dead.

Everything faded to black.

The blackness gave way. I was back where I started five days ago, in that state of neither here nor there. I was surrounded by the purple void, a pink flare off in the horizon like a never rising or always-setting sun.

It was different this time. I had a body. I could see that I was sitting down in a chair. I couldn't feel the coldness or hardness of the metal chair though. It was like my physical sense was just there for aesthetic reasons. I did not feel cold or hot. There was no pleasure or pain. I was just there.

I could hear the sounds of footsteps, and something being dragged toward me. It was the sound of a hard-soled shoe or boot walking on a hard-tiled floor and metal squeaking, even though there was no floor. There were no walls, no ceiling. No sky or ground. No up or down.

From the pink light in the distance, a shadow emerged. I could make out the shape of a woman dragging something behind her. She slowly walked toward me, ever so slowly. The sounds of her footsteps and the dragging and squeaking filled my being. It went on for what seemed like forever, becoming torturous. It drove me mad because there was no logic to the noise. There was no hard floor for her shoes to tap on as she walked. No tile or linoleum for whatever was causing the metallic screeching of the object she pulled behind her. I could not shut the sound out as it became louder and louder. It was drowning me. I felt as if I was being erased as it enveloped me. I sat frozen in my chair with no way to run from it. It just filled me, growing louder and louder. I kept thinking it would break me somehow. Eventually, I wanted it to break me.

After what seemed like an eternity, she was finally in front of me, and everything came to a halting silence. Lilith stood before me for a moment then unfolded the metal chair she was dragging. She sat in front of me, her knees only inches from mine. My mind was still spinning. How long did that last? Seconds? Minutes? Years?

"I know. You're confused," she finally spoke.

I looked around, trying to figure out where I was and what was going on. This had to be a dream. Nothing made sense.

"Whatcha looking for?" she asked.

"Destiny. Where is Destiny?"

Why was Lilith here? Where was here? Was this some sort of Limbo or Purgatory?

"Heck, look at me," she commanded.

I looked back at her. Her smile. That stupid fuckin' grin. How did I not see it before? Hair was different. Eyes were different. Face was different. But that stupid fuckin', spiteful, playful grin was the same.

"You? You're Destiny?"

"In the flesh. Well, you know what I mean," she laughed. "Can't be in the flesh if we're dead, right?"

"Dead?"

"Yes, Heck," she sighed. "You. Me. Dead. This is it."

I stared at her again. Some things were starting to make sense. How her friends and family all reacted when I approached them, looking for her. They would say she was gone. They tried telling me.

I just did not question it. I just assumed gone meant away. It never crossed my mind she was dead.

"What happens now?" I asked. I was still unsure of what my own destiny was.

"This is it," she repeated.

I shook my head. This couldn't be it. It made no sense.

"Look," she sighed. "Remember when I ODed? And you came to see me at the hospital?"

I nodded.

"I told you I died?"

I frowned.

"Well, I was pretty much told what you were told. Only, I didn't have a time limit like you. That was my idea. Pretty good one too," she laughed. "Anyway, I was told I needed to get my shit together because eventually, my time was coming. And depending on how my days on earth were spent was where my eternity would be: Heaven or Hell."

"You had a list of people you needed forgiveness from?" I asked, wondering why I wasn't on her list.

"Oh, no," she laughed. "You and your little list were also my idea. Along with transforming myself into Destiny. Deep down inside, though, you knew it was me."

"Games. You played games with my final days?" This should not have been a surprise to me. It was what Lilith always did. She fucked with people. If the flashbacks and memories taught me anything, she was always fucking with people. We were all pawns in her little games. Especially me.

She shrugged. Her shit-eating grin slowly crept up on her face. I was spiraling, trying to wrap my mind around all of it. From her being Destiny to sitting in this vast void with nothing but the two of us, the clothes on our backs, and the chairs.

"So, now I'm dead. And you're dead. And here we are," she said.

Her voice almost quivered with excitement. She seemed way too happy.

"And just what is here?" I yelled. Even in death, she was so annoying.

"Heck. Think. If Heaven is what made you the happiest, and Hell is what made you the most miserable…" she trailed off, waiting for it to all sink in for me.

And it took me a minute. I had to think. And then, my soul grew cold with dread.

"Lilith, what the fuck did you do?"

"It's what I didn't do, Heck," she smiled. "I didn't forgive you."

It all became so clear to me. I knew exactly where I was. And I knew exactly where Lilith was.

"I got my Heaven," she grinned.

This was it. Lilith and I for our eternity. Only Lilith and me.

"And I got my Hell."

ABOUT THE AUTHOR

Tina Bauer is an up-and-coming author of both novels and children's picture books. Born in Queens, NY, Tina has been writing and telling stories since she was twelve years old. She is now a proud mom of two grown sons, happily married to her best friend, and adores her four-legged babies that complete her family. When Tina isn't creating a story, you can find her cooking, road tripping around the country, reading, sewing, or watching movies.

For more information about Tina and her storytelling journey, follow her on these social media platforms:
Instagram @Tina_b_storyteller
Facebook @Tina Bauer Storyteller
TikTok @Tina_b_storyteller

Tina also occasionally blogs.
You can find her writings at Tinabauerstoryteller.com.